Letters

To

Magnolia

A Maple Small Town Romance Book 1

Cover Design © 2024 Jessica Whaley

Editing by Stevi Kendrick

Jessica Whaley
P.o. Box 785
Leesburg, Al. 35983
authorjdwhaley@gmail.com

ISBN 979-8-218-40524-3 (Paperback)
ISBN 979-8-9906151-0-6 (Ebook)

If life has thrown you shitty curve balls too. This is your reminder to dodge them and keep going.

Prologue

"God, I hate her!"

I hear the familiar voice of my sister in the kitchen of the building where my rehearsal dinner is being celebrated.

I hurried back here to make sure the cake was delivered on time. It was one of the last things unchecked on my list for the perfect night before my wedding tomorrow.

I freeze beside the door trim and listen to what Courtney is saying. Another familiar voice is heard; a male voice.

"It is all going to work out. I promise." That male voice says to my sister and my heart rate accelerates as I realize who it is. Stephen, *my fiancé*.

I step out from the wall keeping me hidden and into the room. My mind is pondering why they are back here alone.

"What is going on here?" I ask them as I look around. My sister's blonde hair is a little frizzy and one of her curls hangs out of place from where it was bobby pinned. She is bigger than I am in the chest area, and I roll my eyes at her strapless pale blue dress. She begged to have a strapless for her maid of honor dress, but I thought it would make her boobs look even bigger. I was right and I am thankful I put my foot down on the decision of straps.

The island in the middle of the kitchen keeps them separated but they both jump when they hear my voice. Neither of them says a word.

"Who do you hate, Court?" I ask my sister sternly.

She shuffles her feet before answering me, "Oh, um, the caterer. She was so rude when she dropped off your cake a few minutes ago." She gestures to the box sitting on the island.

I feel myself relax.

Thank goodness it arrived on time. I walk over to Stephen and kiss him on the cheek. He never looks at me, but I just chalk it up to nerves since this is the last night I will see him before the wedding.

"Isn't he just the best?" I ask Courtney and she smiles at me.

"Yes, he sure is, at everything he does." She smiles and grabs her clutch walking past me and Stephen making her way back out into the main room. I notice as she walks away, her dress is bunched up around her back end and more curls are loose behind her head.

"Did no one tell her that her dress is on wrong, and her hair is a mess?" I giggle as I look at Stephen. He doesn't laugh.

"So, I was thinking," I start to say putting my hands around Stephen's waist, "do I have to stay home? I can get a job. I would very much like to work."

Stephen has told me from day one of getting engaged he wouldn't let me work. I was to be a housewife and raise our future children while he worked. I always dreamed of working somewhere doing things I loved with the people I love. Like a family business.

Stephen huffs, "I've told you time and time again, no. Now drop it." He pulls my arms out from his waist. He turns to leave me in the room alone.

"Oh, what were you telling Courtney everything would be okay about?" I ask following him out.

He rubs his hands through his hair, and I now notice it is messy and not as fixed as it was when we got here.

"I was just telling her not to worry about the cake and the caterer. She wanted to go after the woman for being so rude when she came by." He walks away from me meeting some friends who were standing in the corner.

Huh? I thought to myself. That's odd that Caroline was rude. She is always so loving when I come in to see her at her store or place an order. She may have just been having a bad day.

I take a deep breath and glance around the room. Everyone we know was invited. My parents, mostly my mother, made sure to make this a social event for her as well. I look down at my dress, it is ivory and silk. Simple enough for my taste. The v-cut in the front is just long enough to make it classy but a little revealing. My brunette hair is long and wavy, and my makeup is minimal. Although, if my mother had it her way, I would have had the most on.

Speaking of the devil herself, she glides over to me with a fake smile on her face.

"Ivy, Darling," she kisses my cheek, "have you mingled with your guest and thanked them for coming?" She asks me, but I know it's more like a warning. Our family image is everything to her.

"Yes, Mother." I say tight-lipped, "I have."

She smiles and I fake one back at her, "Ivy, I wish you would have bought the dress I wanted you to have. A little more lipstick would have been better, too."

I ignore her as she stands beside me watching our guest, smiling as some pass by us. I watch as my father is in conversation with some men from his attorney office. He is one of the greats in the southern states. A terribly busy man I see little of. I know he loves us well as he makes sure to tell us often, but I miss the father I had growing up. Sometimes I wish he didn't try to work so hard for my mother to keep up her lifestyle. She is the reason he does it I know but he loves her too much to tell her no.

This wedding tomorrow is mostly about her. Every list I have had, and every box checked, is for her. Disappointing her is like disappointing God himself. She will make sure you feel like you must obey her for if it were not for her, we would not have the life we have. Or so she tells us. It's like my sister and I must constantly stay in her good graces, or she will make sure we are not a part of the family image anymore.

My sister, Courtney, and I are not that close. Though for my mother's sake, I knew better than to leave her out of the wedding party. Courtney and I are just too different. She matches in with this lifestyle more than me.

I watch my sister eye Stephen as he talks to some colleagues and I wonder to myself, *am I really seeing what I think I'm seeing?*

In the kitchen earlier, I thought I felt a connection between the two. My sister and Stephen. I don't know what to think anymore but as I watch her eye him something in my gut tells me to be careful.

"Excuse me, Mother." I say and she nods.

Walking away from her I walk over to Courtney, "Is there a reason you are eyeing my fiancé right now?" I question her.

She laughs, "Oh Ivy, don't be dramatic. I'm eyeing the guy beside him. Corey, isn't it? He's a hunk."

I look over at the two men deep in conversation. I relax and look back at her, "It being our last night at home together," I smile at her, "How about we do like old times and have one last slumber party like when we were kids?"

She huffs and grins at me, "Sorry Ivy, I have other plans tonight. I'll see you at the wedding venue tomorrow!" She walks off from me slowly towards Stephen and Corey.

My father walks up to me and smiles getting my attention away from them, "How is my girl doing?" He asks me proudly.

I give him a big hug around the neck.

"Thank you for all you do, Daddy." I smile to him.

"You are my whole world. I would do anything for you." He hugs me back and tears fill my eyes as I cannot wait for my big day tomorrow.

1

"HOW DID THIS HAPPEN TO ME?" I whisper to myself as tears stream down my face.

I am not sure how long I have been driving but it seems like forever. By the look of my deep ocean blue eyes, freckled face, and interstate signs, I am sure it's been at least a few hours. I know I'm still in the state of Georgia but that is all I know for sure. My long wavy brunette hair is a mess on the top of my head in curls that are halfway up, and half are hanging loose. They were supposed to be brushed out and covered in baby's breath today. I am starting to feel dehydrated from all the tears I've shed, and my head is throbbing with an intense headache.

If it were not for my white Altima, I wouldn't be able to move right now. It's my feet and I am just letting it drive me until I cannot drive anymore. Early this morning, I got on the interstate after running out of my house with nothing but the Nike shorts and t-shirt I had on, my purse, phone and the credit cards in my wallet. Thankfully, I had flip flops on my feet, or I would most likely be barefoot at the moment.

Crap. I say to myself looking down at the blinking low fuel light on my car. I turn at the next exit and pull up to the green Mapco on the left. The place is crowded but thankfully I notice an empty pump on the side closest to the building. Getting out, I take in my surroundings. Just a single gas station sits on the side of the interstate with woods all around.

"Where the hell am I?" I mumble as I look around desperately trying to figure out from the road signs. After a moment, I take out the nozzle and start pumping gas. Leaning back against my car. I watch the numbers go up on the gas pump and I can hear the gas being rushed through the nozzle.

"Pardon me, ma'am." A light female voice says behind me. I turn quickly a little startled. My eyes meet a short dirty blonde hair middle-aged woman looking at me while she's pumping gas on the other side of the pump we share.

I point at myself to make sure she's speaking to me and when she nods, I say, "Yes?"

"Are you lost? You don't look like you are from here?" she gives me a comforting smile.

"I'm actually just passing through." I state with a grin.

"Oh, where are you heading?" she asks.

Dang woman, mind your own business I think to myself but smile at her and answer, "I honestly don't have a destination in mind. I just needed to get away from a situation."

She gasps taking a step back, "You're not running from the law, are you?" her hands covering her mouth.

I roll my eyes at the nosy bitch, "No ma'am." I remember my manners and smile, "Do you know where I can get a good bite to eat? I'm starving." I take the nozzle out and put it back on the pump.

She does the same on her side and once she is done, she proclaims, "Oh honey, you *must* go to Nana's. It's not far from here at all. The cutest restaurant down in Maple! She pulls out her phone and gives me the address. Grabbing my phone from my car, I write the address in my notes and thank her. We both get in our cars as we depart from each other and I let out a deep breath, thankful she wasn't actually inviting me to her family's house to eat when she said, Nana's.

My phone buzzes and I look at the caller I.D.

I roll my eyes. Stephen again.

I hit ignore and type in the address for Nana's in my GPS. Thankfully it's only twelve miles down the road. Pulling out of the gas station parking lot, I follow the GPS to a side road just off the interstate. Putting my phone down in the cup holder my mind floats back to only twelve hours ago. I was at my rehearsal dinner. I was supposed to be getting married right now but instead I don't even know how many miles from home I am. I'm also not even sure if I will ever return.

My whole life I've been trying to please everyone around me and right now it feels like my life is crumbling down. I thought I was checking all the boxes and getting things done. College, *check*. Perfect business degree, *check*. I mean I was going to pay for a brand-new vehicle next week and I had just signed for a brand-new house. Of course I had help from my parents. Mother always made sure she had to approve everything. At twenty-eight years old, I always felt like I was doing everything I needed to have the perfect life. Somehow, I still always felt like the black sheep. The one no one understood and the one everyone tried to dull out.

I never really cared for the lifestyle of luxury. If I had it my way I would be in casual or comfortable clothes most of the time, but my mother would have never let that fly. We were never allowed to leave the house unless we were dressed to impress and have a full face of makeup on.

For the most part, my parents are good people and have always made sure I had everything I could ever dream of. They have always wanted the best for me no matter the outcome. However, being the daughter of one of the greatest lawyers in the southern part of the country, it comes with the pressure of being perfect for our image. How I dressed, how I acted, who I dated, where I went, etc. It all played a part in our life. When I met Stephen, my parents approved immediately because of his family's image and how rich they were. His father was a partner at my father's law firm. I am sure that was a perk for them.

Stephen was in his last year of law school when we met at a business party for our fathers' we were both attending. I fell in love with the idea of checking him off my box for my parents' approval. I knew he didn't love me. Not truly anyway. It did not matter if he did or didn't, I was in love with checking things off for my parents' sake. I think I wanted my mother's approval more than anything.

It wasn't until I walked in on Stephen this morning, *our wedding day*, getting head from my maid of honor - *my sister*, in our new house that I realized just how much I had lsot myself in trying to make everyone else happy.

I wasn't even planning to stop at the house but I forgot some makeup that I had packed still in boxes from moving. Seeing her on her knees at the kitchen table and his hands in her hair was the last thing I expected. I ran out of the door with nothing but my purse, keys, and the clothes I had on. I sat in my car in the driveway crying until I decided to leave. I drove off towards the interstate and my phone has been ringing non-stop since. I cannot bring myself to answer the calls, so I just continue to hit ignore.

"The destination is on your right." The GPS startles me out of the disgusting memory, and I notice the big *WELCOME TO MAPLE* sign as I enter the town limits. Right next door is another big sign that says, *Nana's*. I turn my blinker on and pull into the gravel parking lot. It takes me a moment to find a parking spot because of how busy they are.

Once parked, I look at myself in the rearview mirror, "Well, this is as good as it's gonna get today." I take the last of the curls that are pinned up out of my hair and brush it down.

A tear creases the corner of my left eye and I brush it back. *You are worthy of so much more;* I hear a voice tell me inside my head.

Grabbing the handle to open the door, I let the door open, and I step out. It is the first time I realize how beautiful it is around me. I'm from the city, so we don't get fields like this or blue skies. Around me are cotton fields for as long as I can see, farms with horses and cattle and a tractor just passed by on the main road. There's a fire department next to the town hall I passed coming in and what looks like a bar on the opposite side of the road.

I smile and shake my head at the strange feeling of déjà vu. It almost seems like I have been here before, but I know I haven't. I walk towards the front door and an older man with a hat on and old work clothes starts to walk out. When he sees me, he holds the door open, "Here you go, Miss." He smiles.

"Thank you" I reply with a smile and take the door handle. He gives me a polite smile back and walks off to his car. I assume that is the southern hospitality I have heard about in small towns.

Moving inside the door, I let it shut slowly behind me. There is a sign at the front, next to a bar with a register, that reads, "Sit Anywhere," so I walk on and look around for an open booth. The place is busy with families and couples sitting at the tables. A few children at different tables sit in highchairs and booster seats, giggling. I finally see a booth in the far back and walk over to sit down. The booths are absolutely beautiful. Made of wood and glazed over with some kind of sealer. The tables are wood, too.

"Anyone else joining you?" A young woman walks up to me with a notepad in her hand. She has blonde hair that is pulled back into a loose ponytail. She couldn't be more than her early twenties.

"Just me," I say with a soft smile. "I'm new here, would you happen to have a menu?" I ask.

"Oh, I'm sorry." She starts and points to the buffet bar in the back of the room, "We are buffet only. Everything is made fresh in our kitchen. You can get as many plates as you want. It's only twelve dollars for the buffet per person plus drink. What can I get you to drink?" she asks raising her pen to write.

"Water with no lemon, please." I give her a smile and she returns a nod while walking off to get my drink.

I sit and just watch people for a moment. Older country music plays softly throughout the building. Families, big and small, sit at the table and booths. A few couples sit together laughing and talking. I feel a sense of happiness watching everyone. The workers even look happy, too. The waitress comes back with my drink and sits it down.

She looks at me, "If you need anything just flag me down. I'll be back to check on you. Plates for the buffet are at the bar." I thank her and she walks away.

Standing up from my seat, I walk over to the buffet. There is so much food laid out before me on the buffet and it's all home cooked. Collard greens, baked beans, fried chicken, corn, mashed potatoes, and more. I grab a plate and start eyeing the food in their own sections. It all looks delicious and I'm starving. I start putting a little bit of everything on my plate.

"Whoa, you don't look like you can eat that much." A guy's voice says behind me.

I look up, clearly appalled at what this stranger just said. His brown eyes stare back at me twinkling. He couldn't be more than eighteen or nineteen years old. His dark hair is messy, and his jeans and t-shirt are covered in dirt. I notice he is holding a few to-go bags in his hand.

"Excuse me?" I whip around at him.

His brown eyes widen as they meet mine, "I just meant, I-I, I didn't mean it like that." He says backing away.

I ignore him but he can't seem to get the hint, "Rough day?" he asks me.

I turn again at him and give him a death stare. "What gave that away? My temper or my eyes that are so puffy and blood shot from crying that I look like I've been beat up?" I walk away from him as fast as I can before I have time to react more.

"Sorry ma'am." I heard him say and he walks towards the front door exiting it quickly.

My appetite is now gone. I don't even want to eat but I know I need to, or I'll be sick. I sit down and try to relax by taking a bite of my food and *holy hell*, it's delicious. The most savory food I've ever had, and I get a strange sense of déjà vu again. I feel like I have had this same food before.

Eating until my plate is clean, my phone dings and I look at it. It's a text from Stephen and Courtney. Both apologizing and how sorry they are. They also both said they were worried about me and wanted me to come home so we could talk. I have a missed call from my mother. I sigh. My mom deserves for me to tell her the truth. I'm sure her and my dad are worried sick about me. I was supposed to meet them both at the church this morning. That's where I was heading when I made an unexpected detour to my house.

I text her instead of calling,

I am safe. Just needed to get away. Wedding is off as I'm sure you can imagine by now. I'll call you soon. Trust me, please. I Love you!

My phone dings almost immediately and I ignore it. Putting it back into my pocket the waitress comes back over to me, "Anything else I can get you?" she asks looking at me as if she is worried about me.

"Actually, I was wondering, is there a hotel around here?" I try to ask without sounding too desperate.

"How long are you needing to stay?" she asks me but I'm sure she's just trying to be nosey.

I let out a breath feeling defeated, "I honestly don't know."

She smiles clearing my plates from the table, "Down the road, there's a bed and breakfast. It's called Magnolia Inn. It's old but well taken care of. The family who found the town opened it years ago. Tell the girl at the front desk that Megan sent you." She winks at me.

"And I'm guessing you are Megan?" I smile.

"I am." She nods her head. "Come back tomorrow morning at seven thirty for breakfast, it'll be on the house." She turns and pauses turning back to me, "Your name is?"

I smile, "Ivy. Ivy Price."

Getting up I walk to the front counter and pay for my meal. I don't know how long I'll be able to use these credit cards for. They are in case of an emergency from my parents. I am sure they will try to track me with them.

I sigh. I need to find a way to disappear altogether. Going back is not an option anytime soon. I leave a twenty-dollar tip on the receipt for Megan and walk to my car, typing in the name of the bed and breakfast into my phone GPS and make my way to hopefully a nice place to relax for the rest of the day and night.

2

Magnolia Inn is the cutest bed and breakfast I have ever seen. Which I do suppose other than movies, this is the first one I have ever seen. It's just down the road from Nana's and I'm thankful I didn't have far to drive. Gail, at the front desk, is the nicest lady, and apparently a good friend of Megan's family. There is a beautiful Magnolia tree in the front yard, and I guess that is where the name comes from. Benches and picnic tables line directly under it where it casts the perfect shade for lunchtime or reading hours.

I stayed in my room much of the day yesterday and into the night, only to come out to eat dinner. If circumstances were different, I would read under the magnolia tree or walk around town and explore. It's obvious to others that I am not from here, so I want to keep myself hidden for a little while until I figure out what I'm going to do.

I have no clothes other than the ones I drove to Maple in and I'm sure I reek of body odor, but I get up and make my way back to Nana's to meet Megan for breakfast. When I pull my car into the parking lot, I notice it is as busy as it was yesterday.

Finding a parking spot close to the front, I turn my car off and grab my purse and phone and make my way to the front door. Passing the black Chevy truck that sits beside me a girl comes out from around it, "God, do you not own any more clothes than that?" The girl huffs and turns to me.

"Megan," I cover my chest, "You just scared the shit out of me."

She walks over to me and I notice the sweet girl I saw yesterday has been replaced with a rugged exterior. She's dressed in jeans, horseback riding boots, and a white crop top. Her blonde hair is in a messy bun and her face is clean from makeup.

She takes a step towards me, looks me up and down, and then asks, "What are you actually doing here in Maple, Ivy? You clearly aren't from here." She steps farther into me.

Tears prick my eyes and I quickly wipe one away, "Are we not going to eat breakfast?" I ask trying to avoid her question.

"We will if you tell me the truth." She stares into me sternly crossing her arms over her chest.

I huff letting out all the air in my lungs.

"Yesterday was supposed to be my wedding day. Instead, I found my soon to be husband in my new house cheating on me with my sister who was supposed to be my maid of honor." Tears prick my eyes again and I quickly wipe it away.

She stares at me for a moment as to see if I'm lying and then sighs, "Well, shit. Okay then." Megan turns walking towards her truck.

"*Okay then*?" I ask not moving a muscle.

She opens her truck door, "Get in." she orders me.

Still, I don't move.

"I don't even know you. Plus, you were being very mean to me a moment ago. Why would I go anywhere with you?" I question her, crossing my arms over my chest.

"Because I know how you can start over." She jumps into the driver's seat closing the door.

Shit. Now I'm curious. I look back at the diner and back at her. I'm also freaking starving. Not giving myself another second to talk myself out of it, I double check that my car is locked and open her passenger door.

"Hell yeah!" Megan says and puts her truck in reverse as I slide in and shut the door.

We ride off down the road and pass the inn where I had stayed last night. The town is absolutely breath taking, like something you see in the movie Sweet Home Alabama. Old duplex buildings line the main street full of businesses and the courthouse sits in the middle of it all. Once we got out of the downtown side, it is nothing but cotton fields, farmhouses, barns, pasture and rolling mountains as far as the eye can see. Horses, cattle and tractors roam the fields.

"Are we still going to get breakfast somewhere?" I ask her and she laughs.

"Yes," she rolls her eyes, "You know for such a tiny girl, you sure can put food away." She turns down a dirt road and I notice the columns leading into it. There is a sign that has MAGNOLIA FARM engraved on it. This is someone's driveway.

The road is long, and I wonder if this is where she's taking me to kill me so one no will ever find me. Wooden fence posts and barbed wire fencing line both sides of the driveway as we ride down the dirt road. Horses are running and kicking their heels in the pasture and cows are standing at a hay ring eating their breakfast.

After a moment, the long fence we are driving beside turns into an open field and a beautiful white farmhouse comes into view. It has a wide front porch with porch swing. There is a big, beautiful Magnolia tree beside the house. The people of Maple sure love their Magnolia trees.

Three dogs lay on the porch and perk up as we approach. One of the dogs is a Great Pyrenees. I can tell by the thick white fur. I have read about them online before.

Megan puts the truck in park, and I step out taking a look around. Pastures as far as the eye can see with horses and cattle. Chickens roam the yard and there is a gigantic red barn across the driveway from the house and an old wooden one directly behind the house that looks like it has tractors and equipment in it. There are tulips blooming near the front porch in colors of pink, yellow, and purple. Perfect for a beautiful Spring day.

"Megan," I ask still eyeing the scenery, "Have I died and gone to heaven?"

She laughs and walks towards the front door, "It sure feels like the closest thing to it on Earth, doesn't it?" she pauses, "It's my grandparents' house. My brother and I live here with my grandma. We help her care for the farm." She steps on the front porch and the dogs meet her. I follow behind and the Great Pyrenees comes into my bubble, sniffing me.

"That's Reba." She says, "She's harmless. Unless you're a coyote." She points to what I think is a blue and red heeler, "And these two knuckle heads are George and Izzy." She shrugs, "I'm a big Grey's fan and well you can guess where Reba comes from." I laugh and follow her inside through the screen door. It creaks as it closes behind me.

As soon as we make it inside, my nose is hit with the most captivating smell. Bacon, biscuits, sausage, and gravy are lined up on the table and my mouth instantly waters. An older woman stands at the sink washing her hands and turns when she hears us walk in. She is the magazine cover of what a southern grandmother looks like; Her white hair is pulled up on her head and an apron around her neck. Her glasses are partially down her nose, and she has naturally tan skin from being outside in her garden, I am sure. Her blue eyes look at Megan.

"Meg, so glad you made it in time. Breakfast is ready and I just set the table." She smiles and looks at me.

"Who is your friend?" she asks Megan.

"This is Ivy Price, Grandma. She was passing through and stopped at Nana's yesterday. She's looking for a place to start over." She says winking at me and takes a seat at the table.

The woman stares at me, looking confused, and I walk up and put my hand out. "I am so sorry if I'm intruding." She finally smiles and shakes my hand as if she is remembering her manners.

Megan starts fixing her plate and comments, "She was supposed to get married yesterday but instead found her sister and soon to be husband doing the nasty." Megan informs her without looking up from fixing her plate.

The older woman puts her hand over her heart and gasps, "Oh my dear, I am so sorry. Sounds like your sister is a whore and your fiancé is your *ex-fiancé* I hope?" she winks at me.

I like this woman. I want to be her when I get that age.

"Yes, to both questions. But I haven't spoken to them since I ran out of the house. Everyone is blowing up my phone right now but I don't want to talk to them." I sigh.

She gestures to me to sit, "Sit honey, eat as much as you want, there is plenty. You are welcome to stay here if you need a place to stay." She tells me like it's no big deal. "We can give you a job here on the farm if that's something you would be okay with doing." She states with a grin.

I cough taking a bite from my plate and hearing her words at the same time. "Oh, no ma'am, I wouldn't want to impose." I answer.

"Nonsense." she says waving me off and sitting a glass of orange juice for me to drink.

"Thank you." I reply taking the cup and drinking my cough down.

She continues, "Really, it's no problem. We have the room, and we need the help. This farm takes a lot of work, we have foals being born in a few weeks. Megan can show you the ropes around here." She smiles as she sits down to eat too. "We already planned on finding someone to help. You just made it easy." She laughs. "My name's Margaret, honey. You just let me know if you need anything. You can sleep in the spare bedroom upstairs."

I sit in shock, not really sure what to say.

Bang! I startle in my seat as the screen door flies open and crashes against the door frame as someone enters behind me.

"Smells delicious, Grandma!" the males voice says behind me. He walks closer and pulls his seat out to sit down beside me, his eyes meet mine and they widen.

"*You?!*" I snarl.

"Oh, hell." He says scooting his seat away from me.

Megan points her finger at me and back at the guy. "Y'all know each other?" she asks him confused.

"Not really." He replies.

She looks at him as if she's not buying it, but I help her after I roll my eyes.

"I know all I need to know about him." I say, "He basically told me I was eating too much at Nana's while I was in line fixing my plate."

Margaret gasps and he puts his hands on his hips.

"I said no such thing." He starts, "I just said that I was shocked you ate so much." He says, finally sitting down.

"Collin!" Margaret throws a napkin at him. "Have I not taught you anything over the years?" she snarls at him. "That's no way to talk to a lady."

He looks at me, "She is no lady. I imagine she's The Devil himself with the looks she gives." He starts fixing his plate.

Megan giggles and he looks at her.

"What's so funny?" he asks her with a crooked eyebrow.

"Meet your new farm helper." She points at me.

He drops his fork. Biscuit and gravy fly all over the table, "You've got to be fucking kidding me?"

Megan and I giggle so hard until we are crying and by the look his grandma is giving him, I am quite sure she wants to wash his mouth out with soap.

3

After breakfast, Megan let me freshen up in her bedroom upstairs and change into more appropriate attire for farm work. I feel so much better getting out of my old clothes, even though I am dressed in a pair of her boot cut jeans, a grey tank top and cowgirl boots. It's far from the usual active wear I would normally choose, but I am thankful we are both close to the same size in clothing and have the same shoe size. Running a brush through my hair honestly was the best part of it all. Megan said she would show me around the farm and then take me back to town to get my car and some clothes later.

I meet Megan at the bottom of the stairs in the kitchen and we make our way outside. The dogs follow behind us as we walk to the woodshed behind the house where she jumps on a red Polaris Ranger. I sit down in the passenger seat and pull the cloth door shut on the side. She backs us out of the shed and towards the gate close to the house.

"Newbies open the gate." She says to me with a playful smile. I roll my eyes and get out, "I have a feeling you are going to be a pain in my ass." I joke.

I undo the chain that is looped around the gate and post. Next, I walk the gate open enough where she can drive through, and I shut it back.

Climbing back into the Ranger Megan says, "If no one else is going to make you tough, I will. This world will tear you apart if you let it, Ivy. I'm not going to baby you out here. You deserve to see the strength in yourself. Don't let the world make you forget it." She gives me a soft smile and we head across the open field. The land around us is breathtaking. The grass is green coming to life after Winter and the trees are all fresh with new blooms.

We cross a little creek and I have to grab the handle above me to keep myself balanced. Once we cross over and my eyes widen with a view that takes my breath away. Horses and more horses. I bet there are thirty in the pasture we are in. They are all walking around and grazing without a care in the world that we are here.

Megan stops the Ranger and points at the deep brown colored one in the front whose belly looks like it's about to pop, "We need to bring her in." she says, grabbing the black halter and rope from the back of the ranger.

"What?" I ask while following her, "Why?"

"She shouldn't be out here. I don't know who turned her out. She's due to foal any day now." We walk up to the mare whose head is up now from grazing and watching us approach her. Megan ties the halter around the mare's neck and hands the lead rope to me.

I just stare at it, "What do you want me to do?" I ask her.

"Take this as your first lesson today. Do you want to drive the Ranger back or lead Molly?" she asks.

I look back from the Ranger to the horse in front of me.

"I'll take the Ranger." She nods and I walk off towards it.

"Just go on ahead of me, I don't want the Ranger to spook her. I'll meet you at the gate we came in at." I nod in agreeance putting the Ranger in drive, and start heading to the gate. I see Collin coming through the gate as I get close. He leaves it open, and I drive through. I switch the key off and put on the brake, then jump out to walk back to where he is standing.

"Where's Meg?" he asks me as I get closer to him.

"There was a mare in the field that shouldn't be. Said she was due to foal any day now. She's leading her back." I say propped up on the gate without looking at him.

"Shit. Molly?" he asks me concerned.

"Yeah, she said her name was Molly." I look at him only for a minute then turn my head back to the open pasture. "She didn't know how she got out there." I see Meg coming over the top of the hill with Molly following right beside her.

"She was in her stall when I rounded this morning before breakfast. I checked all the locks. Man, Megan is going to kill me." he states while running a hand through his hair.

I stay quiet as Megan approaches the gate eyeing her brother angrily.

"How is it that we have a very pregnant, due any day, mare in the open pasture? This baby could be a coyote's meal if she would have dropped it out there without us knowing." She says walking past her brother still leading Molly. I follow close behind her.

"I checked all the locks this morning, Meg. I swear, she was in her stall eating hay when I came to breakfast." She ignores him and he gives up walking off to a truck with bales of hay loaded on the bed and drives off.

"Where is he going?" I ask her.

"Going to pick up Logan and take the hay to another farm who bought it from us." She says rubbing Molly's neck as we get closer to the barn.

"I believe him," she finally admits looking at me, "But what kind of big sister would I be if I didn't give my brother hell from time to time?" She winks at me and puts Molly up in her stall while undoing her halter.

Walking over to a bucket, Megan fishes out a lock and puts it around the bar that holds the stall door shut. She points up to the camera at the top of Molly's stall, "This is one of our foaling stalls," she says making sure the lock is secure. "And this little bitch," she points at Molly who sticks out her tongue as if she knows what she is saying, "is a Houdini. I got the alert on my camera while we were cleaning up the dishes from breakfast that she had gotten out and made her way to the back pasture. The gate me and you came through is not the only way out. She went right out the stall and down the opposite hall of the barn, dipped her head right under the fence, and went to where all her friends are." She laughs. "She better be glad for all the awards she has won me through the years and the fact that I love her." She rubs Molly on the nose.

"What did you compete in?" I ask her.

"Barrel racing and break away roping. Molly was my go-to. I cherish many memories on her back." Her smile slowly fades as if she's remembering a sad memory. "We were competing to qualify for the National Finals Rodeo. She fell on the second barrel; I came off and had a concussion and a few broken ribs." She pauses as though the next statement is more painful, "My grandfather wanted to put her down, but I begged him not to. She injured her right leg and we done months of rehab. She has had two surgeries. She won't ever compete again, but she will live her best days in these green pastures and produce babies every other year until I feel like she can't handle that anymore. Then, we will retire her completely and she will live out the rest of her days." She pauses again and tears fill her eyes, "I owe her that much."

I grab her hand and squeeze it, "I'm sure she is so thankful to have you." She smiles back at me.

"Ugh, girl don't make me cry. I still have nightmares about that day." She turns walking down the barn and I follow behind her, "Hey!" she turns to me, "Let's go out tonight!" she puts an arm around my shoulder. "I'm sure you could let off some steam." She grins and hands over to me a shovel pointing to a wheelbarrow.

"What's this for?" I ask and she gives me a smirk.

"You get to clean stalls this week. Have you ever mucked a horse's stall before?" she cocks an eyebrow at me.

I shake my head no. Megan points to the stalls behind me and I walk over and start looking in them. My eyes widen with horror.

"Oh, you cannot be for real?" I whisper, standing in shock.

She laughs, "I told you I'm going to make you tough before it's over with." She walks into the tack room and comes walking out with a halter.

"Having you here will give me time to ride some colts without having to worry about all the million things I have to do. It's not as bad as you think." She pauses and puts the halter over her shoulder, "Just holler at me if you need anything, I'll be in the arena." She points to an outside pen out in the pasture as she walks to a stall and brings a horse out with her.

I choose the stall next to a big brown color horse who keeps staring at me like he's wondering what the hell I'm doing here, too.

Great. Even the horses know I don't belong here.

4

I have never seen anything more unattractive in my life as I stand in front of the mirror in the spare bedroom looking at myself. The jeans I'm wearing are covered in horse shit and dust. My hair is tangled all over the bun I have it up in. My face has dirt all over it making me look like I've crawled in mud all day. My legs and arms are so sore. I don't think I've worked so hard in all of my life.

After putting Molly up, Megan put me to work. She told me she was going to give me easy work today. If mucking stalls and feeding hungry animals is the easy work, I'm worried my time here will be worse than driving back home and facing the things I'm running from. I sigh taking my hair down from my bun.

Megan peaks her head in the door and says, "You did good today for someone not used to this kind of life."

I turn to face her and say, "I am going to be so sore tomorrow." I halfway laugh. "Where are we going tonight? I don't have clothes." I tell her.

She waves me off, "Get cleaned up and come in my room. I'm sure there's something in my closet that will fit you. We are going to Hilltop! It's a bar in town. Shower is available. Towels are in the cabinet under the sink. You can use my shampoo and conditioner in there. Hurry before Collin gets in. He hogs all the hot water." She rolls her eyes at the thought of her annoying brother and leaves me.

Opening the door to the bathroom, I first notice how clean it is. It looks exactly like I'd picture a farmhouse bathroom to look like. Pictures of horses and cows decorate the walls and there is only a single sink, toilet and tub-shower combo with a shower curtain covered in horses, as well. I quickly strip out of my clothes and look around for a laundry basket to put them in. Opening the closet door, I see a hamper to throw my clothes in while walking over to the shower and turn it on.

Stepping into the shower I stand and let the warm water hit me for a few minutes. Dirt rolls off me and the water going down the drain quickly turns to mud. I take in a deep breath and exhale, letting the weight of the work today leave my tired muscles as I focus on getting cleaned up.

The sound of the bathroom door opening makes me jump and I pull the curtain back to where only my head peaks out keeping my body covered.

My heartrate speeds up and my eyes widen when I see Collin stepping inside. He has earphones in his ears loud enough that I can hear the music, which means he can't hear the water going in the shower. He doesn't notice me because he is too busy staring into his phone. Walking over to the toilet, he starts to unbutton his jeans to sit. I gasp. *Oh no*. He's about to take a shit! I yell at him, but he keeps his phone in his hands scrolling on it. He eases himself down on the toilet and I start to panic. Looking around the shower, I pick up the bottle of shampoo and throw it at him.

He jumps and looks up.

His eyes widen, "Oh. My. God." He screams and jumps up pulling his pants up quick. Megan comes running in and she covers her mouth, "Collin!" she screeches at him, "What the actual fuck, dude?" she says, eyeing him.

He stands away from me but puts his hands over his eyes too. "I didn't see anything." He screams. "I just need to take a shit. I had my air pods in my ears." He's so embarrassed. Megan and I look at each other and start laughing.

"Sorry." She mouths to me, and she grabs her brother by the shirt and pulls him out of the bathroom and closes the door.

Note to self: Next time, lock the door.

***

I feel like a new woman after my shower. Wrapping my hair in a towel, I pull another one around my body securing it under my arms, I look in the mirror and smile. *You can do this.* Opening the door, I head to Megan's room.

She is sitting in front of her makeup mirror, and she turns as she hears me step in, "Here are some skinny jeans. Those boot cuts you wore today fit you perfectly." She says throwing me her jeans. "How do you feel about crop tops?" she asks me.

"What happened to rough and tough, Meg?" I laugh. She's acting girly, nothing like the girl I have seen today. She smirks and says, "A girl can be both tough and a lady." She reaches into her closet, "Plus, it keeps the boys guessing which one they are going to get. They know better than to mess with you that way." she tosses a crop top to me.

"This is short." I look over it with widening eyes.

"That's the point." She smiles. "We need you to forget about the shitty past couple of days you've had. Let loose tonight and just have fun. Let the people of Maple help you feel loved!" she smiles going back to her makeup chair picking up her mascara.

"Megan?" I say in almost a whisper.

She looks up at me through the mirror, "Huh?"

"Thank you for being a friend. I don't have any girlfriends back at home. They all left me once they got married or had babies. It's nice having someone who is helping me get through this time." I smile at her.

"I've got your back girl." She gives me a soft smile.

I turn to walk out the door and stop, turning back to her, "Oh, can I use some of your makeup and maybe a hair dryer?" I gesture to my face and hair.

She throws back her head in a laugh, "Yes but tomorrow we go shopping for you some clothes and your own shit." She gets up to hand me her hair dryer. I nod and walk out of the room with a pep in my step.

Staring at myself in the mirror in the spare bedroom, I feel like myself again. The skinny jeans fit perfectly, and I have them paired with some of Megan's boots. The crop top she gave me actually makes my boobs look great, considering I am a part of the itty-bitty titty community. My hair is down and in loose curls and I put just a small amount of makeup on, focusing more on my eyes making them not look as puffy from crying as much as I did yesterday.

"Let's go!" Collin hollers from the bottom of the stairs. I roll my eyes and grab my wallet, stick my phone in it, and walk out of the room.

"You know I actually begged my parents to return him when he was born?" Megan snarls walking out of her room.

I giggle. "He's coming with us?" I ask confused.

"Someone's got to be the D.D." she winks. "He's six months away from twenty-one and even though the folks there wouldn't say a word, I use it to my advantage." She shrugs.

"If he's almost twenty-one, how old are you?" I ask her.

She grins, "Twenty-four. Almost twenty-five."

I nod and we make our way down the stairs.

"Ivy, I am so sorry!" Collin says still looking embarrassed.

I smile, "I'm just glad you didn't stink up the place." Patting him on the shoulder. Megan bends over in a hoarse laugh. Collin looks at me with wide eyes as we walk past him.

"Where are you kids going tonight?" Margaret asks from the kitchen table while writing in a notebook.

"Hilltop." Megan says leaning down to kiss Margaret's cheek. "Don't worry, we won't be out late, and I have the foal alert on to alert me if Molly starts foaling. I'm still waiting on her to wax so it may be a few more days." She pats her grandma's shoulder.

I smile at her, and she smiles back, "Enjoy yourself tonight, Honey. You need to remember who you are." She goes back to writing.

Collin walks over and kisses his grandma bye on the cheek and the three of us walk out of the door and to his truck. It is an older square body dark green single cab Chevrolet. Collin jumps in the driver's side, Megan slides in to the middle and I climb in the passenger side. "My Give a Damn's Busted" by Jo Dee Messina starts playing on the radio and Collin goes to turn it, "Touch it and you die!" Megan says, grabbing his hand and turning it up. "Ivy, this is the motto for tonight." She screams, "IVY'S GIVE A DAMN IS BUSTED" She nudges me, making me giggle away the tears prickling at my eyes.

Heading back into town, businesses are closed for the night and the streetlights are lit up along main street. We pass Maple Town Hall and it's a beautiful red brick building with Maple trees all out front. Up on the left the sign for the bar is brightly lit, with a large parking lot and a good-sized building in the middle of it. The neon pink open sign is lit up and you can hear music coming from the inside.

"Tonight, you're going to let loose and forget that piece of shit ever existed." Megan says grabbing my hand and walking us towards the door. Collin gets to the door first and holds it open for us, "Such a gentleman." I smirk at him, and he salutes me.

The smell of cigar smoke hits me as soon as I walk through the door. A large bar is along the entire back wall looking almost identical to the bar from Coyote Ugly. Collin walks off from us walking to a group of guys that he noticed. A huge dance floor takes up the middle and it is lined with round tables and four pool tables to the side.

I follow Megan up to the bar, "Hey Joey!" she yells at the older long-bearded guy behind the bar. "This is my girl, Ivy. She's new here but whatever she gets put it on my tab." She winks at him, and he nods.

I grab her shoulder and turn her towards me, "No way, I can't let you pay for all my shit. I feel like I been mooching off of you as it is." I say to her with wide eyes.

She waves me off, "Don't worry about it, besides come tomorrow, you'll hate me again anyways. You have more stalls to clean." She laughs at me looking not so happy about my chores I will be doing now.

"What can I get you ladies?" Joey, the bartender asks us.

"Michelob Ultra." Megan says to him, and he nods picking up a bottle and twisting the top off handing it to her.

"And you, Miss?" he asks turning to face me.

"Umm," I stare looking at all the options listed on the wall. Stephen never allowed me to drink. He always told me it would ruin our image and we needed a clean image. I look back at Megan and give an "I don't know" look.

She nods as if understanding, "Give her the same." She tells him and he grabs me a bottle, twists off the top, and hands it to me. We thank him and I follow Megan as she walks to a table with empty seats. Sitting down and taking a sip of her drink, she turns to me, asking, "Have you never drank before?"

I gulp, "Wine here and there at home when I was alone." I pause before finishing. "Stephen never wanted me to drink. He always told me it made our image look bad and we didn't need to lower our standards." I sigh before saying my last thought. "It was always easier to let him do what he wanted than to argue. There was no winning an argument with him." I take a bigger sip of my beer than I had intended. To my surprise, I actually like it.

Megan huffs, "Your first mistake, Ivy, was letting him get away with being a prick." She takes another sip of her drink.

"You need another one." She says pointing to my already almost empty beer. Before I have time to argue, she's making her way over to the bar grabbing us more drinks.

I'm going to regret all of this in the morning, but after four beers, I feel more myself than I have in years. Megan ordered a plate of loaded nachos when she went back the second time to get us more drinks. I think she was afraid I was going to be sick.

"I haven't been this relaxed in a while." I tell her diving into the plate of nachos in front of me. She laughs and says, "Maybe I should have gotten you a plate for yourself." I grin at her.

The dance floor gets crowded as "Boot Scootin' Boogie" comes on the surround sound and people make their way crowding the dance floor. All of a sudden, everyone starts line dancing. I am mesmerized by the way they all move.

"Let's go dance!" I say jumping up from my seat and looking at Megan.

"Oh, no. I don't dance." she says sternly. "You go ahead, have fun!" she says gesturing to the floor. I take another sip of my beer and run off to the floor jumping into the line and moving right along with them. Another sense of déjà vu comes over me again. I shake off the feeling in my gut and start rocking my hips back and forth and dancing along with everyone to the music. I mess up a few times and giggle at myself. Everyone else does it with such ease. I look up and Megan is whooping and hollering at me, being my biggest hype girl. I laugh and stick my tongue out at her and keep dancing, feeling freer than I have in years.

The song comes to an end and people start to exit the dance floor. I see Collin and another guy walk over and sit down at the table Megan and I were sitting at. The guy sitting with them looks closer to my age and he's tall. His chestnut brown hair is cut short, and his muscles are busting out of his green button up shirt. I walk back to our table. "City girl has moves," Collin says throwing his hands up and rocking back in his chair mimicking me dancing. I pop him on the head, and he holds his hands blocking me.

"Hey!" he says to me, and I grin walking to my seat and sit down.

"Logan," Megan says to the other guy at the table, "This is Ivy, she's new in town and new hired help on the farm."

His green eyes look me over and nods tipping his beer to me and then taking a sip, "You ever worked on a farm before?" he asks me.

"Not util today. Megan had me mucking stalls all day." I take a sip of my drink.

He laughs as if what I said was naive and puts his beer down with a thump so loud, I jump. "I thought I told you we needed a man for help?" He says to Megan to avoid looking my way.

"Excuse me?" I say before Megan has a chance to answer.

"You've done did it now." Collin says looking amused.

"You heard me, little girl. You don't look like you could throw even one bale of hay much less a trailer full. Are you able to wrangle a calf if you need to? My guess is no." he says eyeing me strongly.

"Children," Megan says sternly, "Enough! Grandma was happy about the decision and her decision is final. Ivy has had a rough few days. She could use a change of scenery." She says eyeing Logan.

He huffs and I turn to him, "Wait, please don't tell me I have to work with you."

He grins looking at me from the corner of his eye.

"Every day, seven days a week, Sweetheart." He snarls.

"My name is not *Sweetheart*." I growl at him.

He smirks, "Honey, I don't care what your name is as long as you can hold your own weight out there."

He takes one of my nachos and pops it into his mouth.

"Say please." I say and it catches him off guard.

"What?" he asks confused.

"You took one of my nachos and didn't even say please." I point my finger at him.

"Dude, she's weird about food. Just do it." Collin says to Logan.

I eye Collin, "Don't you even fucking start." I point my finger at him and then back to Logan. Collin throws his hands up in surrender.

Logan smirks and takes another nacho putting it in his mouth, grinning from ear to ear.

Without another thought, I pick up my beer and pour it all over the top of his head.

"What the fuck?!" he says growling at me.

"You didn't say please." I answer smiling at him, pleased with myself and sitting back down in my seat.

Megan and Collin both start cackling. Collin looks like he is about to fall out of his seat. "I told you man, she's weird about her food." Collin hands Logan a napkin.

"You will pay for this tomorrow." Logan states rubbing the napkin across his face.

I lean in towards him and grin, "Bring it on." Easing a nacho into my mouth while smirking back at him.

5

I wake up to the smell of biscuits and gravy with a side of a pounding headache. I'm in my bedroom and still in the clothes I went to the bar in. I sit up. *Shit.* I grab my head and turn to the nightstand to grab my phone. A water and a bottle of Tylenol lay by my phone. I take one and drink some of the water.

Slowly standing up out of bed I catch a glimpse of myself in the mirror across from the bed. Yikes. I look like I've been ridden hard and put up wet. A pair of jeans and a tank top is laying over the chair beside the mirror with a note; *We will go get you some clothes after chores this morning. Put these on. – Meg.*

I smile. I'm thankful to have found such a good friend since ending up here. I change clothes quickly and throw my hair up in a messy bun. Walking down the stairs I hear laughter and conversation at the kitchen table.

"Morning, Sunshine." Margaret says to me as she sits biscuits down on the table.

I grunt holding my pounding head, "Someone is a light weight." Megan laughs fixing an orange juice. I grunt again sitting down in the seat beside her.

Looking up I realize there's an extra person sitting at the table, my eyes widen when I realize he's snarling at me. "I'm guessing drunk me gets angry quick?" I shrug trying to give a sweet smile.

Hc snarls, "You will work the back forty with me today." He says taking a bite of his food. "So, eat up, Buttercup. You'll need your strength."

Megan looks at him, "Now, Logan, you know that is not the place for her to be right now. She will get hurt." She shakes her head at him as if silently telling him no.

Margaret looks at him with her hands on her hips, "Logan, what is this about?" she asks while pointing back and forth at us.

He huffs, "Someone decided to pour her beer all over me last night."

"Well, someone took my food without asking nicely." I whip at him.

Margaret grins, "Nah, Megan. I think you're wrong. This one has a fire in her. Kind of reminds me of myself when I was her age." She sits down at the head of the table. "I think it's a lovely idea."

I smile at her and nod, thankful for the support.

"Have you ever ridden a horse?" Collin asks me.

I freeze, "No."

Logan laughs, "Well, today you get to."

I drop my fork in my plate, and everyone giggles.

***

Logan and I are standing in the hall of the barn with two horses tied up waiting to be saddled.

"This is Tiny." He says patting the horse on the neck. He is a large brown horse with a long dark mane.

"He is what we call our babysitter. He is our most trusted gelding. He normally hauls the kids around when we are giving lessons but today, he can babysit you." Logan jokes.

I roll my eyes at his remark.

"What are we doing with them?" I ask him.

"We are checking fences and making sure there aren't any new calves in the pasture who need to be brought in." He throws a pad and saddle over Tiny, and I watch as the stirrups fall to his sides and a long pad hangs low.

"This is called your girth." Logan instructs me, "it goes under his belly to keep your saddle secured."

He cinches his girth up on the other side. When he's done, he does the same to his horse. He walks into the tack room and walks back out with two bridles and two ropes.

"Why do we need ropes?" I ask, confused.

He chuckles, "You seriously don't know anything do you, city girl?" he places a rope around each of our saddle horns. He turns to me and hands me a pair of gloves.

"Here, put these on." He turns walking to Tiny and putting the bit in his mouth, "In case we have to rope a calf to bring it in. The back forty is about 80 acres across the pound. You never know what we might get into." He puts bags on the back of the saddle and ties them to it. Sticking a few waters and crackers in the bags. "In case you get hangry." He says with a smirk, jokingly.

"Such a gentleman." I roll my eyes.

He walks both horses over to the end of the barn and wraps his reins around his. She stands there politely while he helps me.

"Okay," he starts, "I'll boost you up, just put your foot in that stirrup, and pull up with the horn."

I nod, "Any excuse to touch my ass huh?" I laugh.

"Believe me, it's not my type." He smirks as I pull up. He pushes and helps me throw my other leg over. I freeze. Tiny is a big horse, a lot taller than he looked from the ground.

"Hang on, I need to adjust your stirrups," Logan says placing his hand on my thigh and I jump at the touch. He notices that he's touching me and removes his hand quickly. "That should do it." He says after adjusting the back of it to let the stirrup out some and I place my foot back into it. He was right, it feels so much better now.

"You are going to have to relax, Ivy. Tiny will take care of you. He knows this place like a tracking dog. I wouldn't put you on anything that wouldn't take care of you." He says to me, pulling himself up on his mare.

I nod but don't say a word. I feel Tiny shift under me, and I jump. "What is he doing?" I exclaim a little louder than I expected.

"Relax," Logan says, "he's getting flies off his leg. He will follow me most of the time. Just pull back on the reins in your hand if he's going too fast for you." He kicks his mare and walks off in front of me. Tiny follows. I tense up and hold on to the horn so tight the veins in my hands are visible.

After a moment, I relax and take in the beautiful scenery around me. The mountains and sky are so beautiful, and the grass is flowing with the tiny breeze the morning has given us. I'm in awe and look down at Tiny. He is a magnificent creature. To think, today I was supposed to be on my honeymoon in the Caribbean. Instead, I am on a beautiful ranch with beautiful animals doing things I have never done before.

Logan's mare crosses over a creek and he turns around and says, "Let him do the work. You just hold on and lean back as he crosses the ditch." I nod and Tiny does exactly that. Such a smooth cross and I reach down and pat him on the neck.

We are riding side by side as logan is the closest to the fence line and I'm on the outside watching what he's doing. He's checking the barbed wire making sure its still intact.

"How long have you been doing this?" I ask him.

He is silent for a moment as if he's unsure if he wants to discuss this and then says, "About five years. I came here looking for work after my mother and father died. Collin and Megan's grandfather gave me a job." He says without looking at me.

"Oh, I'm sorry. Is there anyone else in your life other than the people you found here?" I ask and we stay quiet for a little while longer.

"I did have a girlfriend. But we broke up after my parents died. I wanted a fresh start after I met Mr. Jefferey, Margarets husband." He finally answers me.

I was about to ask about their grandfather, but he cuts me off, "How did you find this place?"

I laugh and he looks at me like he doesn't realize what is funny.

I sigh and explain, "It was random. I was supposed to get married two days ago. But, the morning of my wedding, I found my soon-to-be husband getting head from my sister." I laugh to keep the tears from forming.

He stares at me, no emotion on his face. It makes me feel like I should keep talking so I go on, "I got in my car, hysterically crying," I sigh, kind of embarrassed, "and I hit the interstate. A few hours later, I ended up here. I walked into Nana's diner and Megan was my waitress. She offered me free breakfast the next day and brought me here." I stop and look at him to see if he's even following and he is still staring at me. So, I go on, "and now, the day I'm supposed to be in the Caribbean on my honeymoon, I am on the back of a horse, checking fences with a grumpy dude, doing more work than I've ever done in my life. It's so random." I laugh again.

Logan doesn't say anything and turns to look at the land before us. My breath hitches as I realize we are on top of the mountain. I can vaguely see the farmhouse and the barn at the bottom. The sky is so blue, and the grass is multiple colors of green. The birds chirp around us and I watch as cattle are just ahead of us. Calves are playing and running around their mothers.

"There's no such thing as random." Logan finally says and it catches me off guard. He never looks my way, but I stare at him. Half of me feels like he's not as grumpy as he shows himself to be.

Something up ahead gets my attention and I look at Logan, "Do you hear that?" I ask him.

"No?" he says looking to where I'm pointing. "What does it sound like?"

I don't answer him, instead my body reacts before my brain can and I kick Tiny in the sides. He takes off trotting first and then opening up into a lope. My muscle instantly starts moving along with his rhythm. Again, I get a weird sense of déjà vu.

Coming to a flowing creek I pull Tiny to a stop and Logan comes riding up behind me. "Jesus, Ivy. You can't just take off like that, you will scare the cattle." He says angrily at me. I ignore him, hearing the sound again and this time it's louder. Logans head shoots towards the direction of the sound.

"Shit." He says, "That's a calf in distress."

My heart starts hammering in my chest and he kicks his mare taking off towards the area we heard it. Tiny instantly follows behind him.

We get up to a creek and I hear rushing water. The creek is much bigger than the one we crossed to get here. It looks deep and is flowing rapidly with a current.

He stops as we get close and says, "There!"

I see what he is pointing at. A dark brown calf is stuck on a rock in the middle of the creek. Its hoof just barely hangs over the rock to keep it from floating down the stream. It is soaked and its eyes look almost nonexistent. There is a brown color heifer with a white stripe on her face standing at the edge of the creek hollering out, jumping back and forth. It must be the mother.

"That's a newborn." Logan says, "Couldn't be more than a few hours old." He pulls out his phone calling someone and says, "Collin, quick. Grab Meg, we have a calf stuck in the large creek in the back forty," he pauses. "For fuck's sake, hurry, and bring the pistol." He hangs up in a hurry and grabs his rope off his horn.

My eyes widen, "W-why a gun?" I ask.

But as soon as the words leave my mouth I see why. A coyote has emerged from the tree line on the opposite side of the creek from us. It's stalking its way towards the calf. My heart rate speeds up, and I think I might vomit.

"Ivy, I hate to put you on the spot, but I don't have a choice. We have got to get to the calf before the coyote does." He says, not looking at me but his voice is shaky.

"O-oh, okay." I stutter. "Tell me what to do."

"It'll take Collin and Meg at least a few minutes to get here after they saddle up. I need you to hold my weight with Tiny. I'm going to loop the lasso around me and wade into the water. When I tell you to, you pull Tiny back. He will pull us out."

My eyes widen, "Logan, it's too dangerous. What if I mess up?"

He looks at me with emotion in his eyes, "Nothing's random, remember? We are here for a reason. You found this farm for a reason. You heard this calf for a reason." He jumps down off his mare and wraps his reins around her neck. She stands still.

"The gloves you have on will protect you from getting rope burn, once the lasso is around my waist, I want you to wrap it as hard as you can around your horn. Hold your end as tight as you can, okay? Follow me until you get to the edge of the water and then release tension until I tell you to pull us out. Whatever you do, don't let go."

I nod, taking a deep breath trying to lower my heart rate. *Ok, Ivy, you can do this,* I say to myself. Logan loops the lasso around his waist, and I walk with him closer to the creek. The coyote stops in his tracks but does not run off.

"Watch me but keep your eye on him, too." Logan says pointing to the coyote. I nod.

"Talk to me, Ivy, I need to know you understand." He orders me.

"I understand." I say back at him, and he turns and starts walking into the creek. My firm hand is on the rope and once I start to feel tension, I wrap it around the horn as tight as I can allowing Tiny to walk towards the creek. I make sure a little bit is left to hang so Logan can walk without pulling him backwards. Mama cow has switched from hollering to now, pacing the area. It's as if she understands that we are here to help. I am amazed how she trusts us.

Logan is almost waist deep in the creek and finally makes it to the rock. "How is the calf?" I yell at him.

He unhooks the foot that is around the rock and pulls the calf to his chest. "It's alive but not looking good. We need to get it to the barn and warmed up." He says turning back to face me, "Okay, Ivy, now slowly back Tiny up." He says and I do as I'm told. Tiny listens to me as I'm pulling back on the reins and starts slowly backing up. I can hear hoof beats coming up the hill from behind us. I look over my shoulder to see if I can see them, but they haven't made it over the top yet. When I turn back to face Logan and the calf, the coyote darts towards them at full speed.

"Logan!" I scream and he turns around to see it too.

"DRAG US OUT!" he hollers at me as I pull tension on the rope and pull on my reins telling Tiny to move back faster.

BANG.

Ringing sounds in my ears and I see the coyote drop dead in a split second.

I look beside me, and Megan is holding a shot gun up on her shoulder. I let out a big breath and Logan makes his way out of the creek completely. He quickly looks over the calf checking for any sign of injury.

Mama cow walks over to sniff and lick her baby. "Good Mama." Logan tells her. My heart swells with happiness seeing the mama interact with her newborn calf.

"We need to get it to the barn," Megan starts, "Have you checked if it's a boy or girl?"

Logan wipes his soaked jeans with his hands and says, "Nope. Been too busy trying not to die." He gives her a look and Collin snickers.

"Are you okay?" Logan asks turning to me. "That was a lot to ask of you." He says taking the rope from my shaky hands.

"I'm just glad that baby is safe." I say with tearful eyes watching it and its mama.

"It'll ride back with me. You follow and make sure mama stays with us. She should follow us back since we have it. We will need to milk her to get the colostrum for the baby." I nod at him, and he picks up the calf like it's a feather and places it in front of his saddle. He then climbs up and lays it over his lap.

"Ready?" he asks me, and I nod. We turn around following Megan and Collin back to the house. I turn my head back to see the coyote lying there dead. I cannot believe I was supposed to be in the Caribbean right now. Logan is wrong, everything is definitely random.

6

What do you mean the card declined?" I ask the cashier.

"I'm sorry, Miss. It just tells me it's declined." she replies to me regretfully.

I turn to Megan, "That's impossible. This is my parent's credit card. They gave it to me in case of any emergencies." Tears prick my eyes.

We came to town after we got back with the calf. She could tell I was emotional and needed to step away, so we offered to grab lunch for everyone while Logan and Collin finished checking over the calf and doing chores. I was going to pick up my car and bring it back to the farm with us since it was still at Nana's.

"Suzie," Megan says turning to the woman, "Put it on my tab." The cashier smiles at Megan and gives me a sympathy smile and bags my clothes.

"Megan," I say with tears in my eyes, "I cannot let you do this."

The cashier hands us the bag with at least a hundred dollars worth of clothes and I won't grab it. Megan rolls her eyes and grabs it instead, "Oh it's no big deal, girl. You pulled your own weight this morning on that mountain. This is my thank you." She smiles grabbing my hand and pulling me out of the store.

We walk in silence along the main street in Maple heading towards Nana's to pick up our to-go order for lunch. I have never seen a town so beautiful and simple. Everyone we pass says hello and all of them know Megan.

"This town is so beautiful." I state in awe.

She smiles. "I'm thankful to call it home."

"Is your grandfather still alive?" I ask her.

She pauses as if the statement stung her a little and she nods. "He has Alzheimer's. A few years ago, Grandma put him in the nursing home a few towns over because he got to be too much to handle along with the farm. She was afraid he would hurt himself."

I nod in silence as we cross the street walking towards Nana's. It's a beautiful day and the flowers are blooming all over town. Nana's is always busy with little parking left in in the parking lot.

A gentleman holds the front door open for us. "Good evening, Meg. Your grandmother's lunch is the best," he says to Megan, and smiles at me letting the door go as we walk in.

I turn to Megan, "Your grandmother also cooks here?" I ask stunned. She laughs, "She doesn't just cook here, she owns it." She says nonchalantly. "You didn't taste the similarity when you ate at the house?" She walks behind the buffet and back to the kitchen.

I follow her. "I mean, yeah but also, no. I suppose I never put it together. Is that why you were here the day that I was, and you haven't been since I've been at the farm?" I ask her as she hands me the to go plates sat back for us.

"Yeah," she looks around and grabs a few rolls from a fresh pile and wraps them up, "They needed extra hands that day. One of the waitresses called in sick so I took her spot. I don't normally work here but I help out at times." She smiles saying hey to a few of the workers then leading us back to the front of the building telling everyone bye.

"Why is it called Nana's?" I ask after a moment, "All I hear you and Collin call her is Grandma."

She stays quiet for a bit, and we look both ways before crossing the street then she says, "To be honest, I'm not sure. It may have been named that when she bought it or something and just kept it the original name. She owned it before I was born."

I'm quiet with nothing more to say. Then as if a memory jogs my brain, I say, "Crap! I need to call my parents. I have no money if I can't use the card." I pull my phone from my purse and realize the signal is gone. I turn it to

Megan, "Does this mean what I think it means?" I ask with a sigh.

"Damn," she says, "Is that on Stephen's plan or your parents?" she asks.

I huff out a deep breath, "My parents. Stephen and I planned to go get new phones as soon as we were back from our honeymoon."

"That's tough," she says to me as we reach her truck, "I don't know what I'd do until I was in the situation, but I'd at least want my child to be able to get in touch with me if they needed to, no matter the situation or their age." She shrugs to me. "I'm sorry. You can use the house phone to call them when we get back."

I wipe away a tear, "I don't know what I'd ever do if I had not found you and this place."

She gives me a hug and I put the plate of food I was carrying in the passenger seat of her truck. I'll follow her home in my Altima.

***

We both pull up at the house and make our way to the front porch with lunch. I notice

Margaret writing in her book at the kitchen table through the screen door. We startle her as Megan opens the door and she closes her book getting up from her seat, "Oh girls, back so soon?" she smiles putting the book away in a drawer. "How was the restaurant?" she asks Megan while taking the to-go plates from us.

"Good and busy." She tells Margaret with a smile.

"I had no idea that was your place!" I tell her, "Your food is the best. But how are you here and not there cooking?" I ask confused.

She laughs, "Oh honey, I cook in the mornings but once we got busier, I hired chefs and taught them my recipes." She winks at me, "An old lady like me can't do everything these days."

I smile at her.

"Heard you had an interesting morning…" she eyes me, and I shuffle my feet. "I just did what I was told." I explain to her.

"To hear Logan talk, he couldn't have done it without you." She grins grabbing plates to sit at the table.

"Where are the boys?" Megan asks her while looking around. "Oh, I see Collin," she says looking out the window, "I'll go get them." I nod and stay in the kitchen with Margaret.

Once Megan is out of sight, I turn to Margaret and ask, "May I use your phone. Mine apparently isn't working."

She looks up at me from placing napkins on the table and points to the living room, "It's in the den." She says, "Use it anytime you need it, honey."

I thank her and walk into the living room. It's a cute little room, full of pictures of years passed and little figurines. There's a grandfather clock that sits on the far back wall. Beside the couch is a corded telephone and I smile at it. I haven't seen one of these in years. Sitting down on the couch, I pick up the phone and dial the number I've been dreading since I got here. My mother.

Ring. Ring. Ring.

"Hello?" my mother's voice rings on the other end of the line.

"Mom?" I ask in a quiet voice.

"Ivy!" she gasps, "Where on earth are you? Your father and I have been worried sick." I hear noises in the background. "Stephen and Courtney are worried about you too. They are here, now."

I close my eyes. Perfect timing.

"Mom, I'm fine. I need time to figure out what I want to do." I pause, "I called because my credit card declined earlier, and my phone is no longer working." There's a long pause at the end.

"Yes, well, we thought if we cut off your means, you would come back home." She sounds proud of herself.

I huff, "We?"

She clears her throat, "Well, your father has been working a lot trying to clean up your mess. But I took it upon myself to cut you off until you return to your senses."

I roll my eyes. Typical of her. "What if there was an emergency? What if I needed it?" I say louder into the phone.

She clears her throat again, "Should have thought about that when you embarrassed our family name and didn't show at your wedding day."

I can't believe what I'm hearing.

"Mom, Stephen was cheating on me - with my own sister!" I yell into the phone.

She answers sternly, "No, what you saw was a misunderstanding. But even if you did see what you think, they are sorry and say it will never happen again. He loves you, Ivy, and his family is very wealthy. Where are you? I'll have your father send a car for you."

I can hear Stephen's voice in the background. "Tell her I will buy her a brand-new car if she comes home."

Anger takes over me and I scream into the phone with all of my breath, "FUCK ALL OF YOU!" My voice cracks and I have to take a breath. "I won't be coming back home anytime soon if even at all."

Tears run down my cheek, "If that is how you feel." My mothers harsh tone says on the other end, "I'm disappointed in you, Ivy. If finding yourself is what you need, then so be it. But don't come crying back to me when you realize I am right."

I throw the phone down on the receiver ending the call without a goodbye. Being able to slam a phone rather than just hit the end button felt good, but not good enough to stop what was about to happen. I feel the emotions flooding in and I throw my head into my hands. I want to scream but instead tears flow from my eyes. None of them care about me or how it affects me, all they care about is their own well-being.

The cushion next to me dips and someone wraps their arms around me. The embrace makes me cry harder.

"Shhh, shhh," I hear Margaret's voice tell me, "You are welcome here for as long as you need." I lift my hands and look at her, she wipes away one of my tears, "No boy is worth crying over sweetheart. And the one that is won't make you shed one single tear. *Unless* it's from an orgasm." She winks at me. I half-heartedly laugh.

"That's the spirit," she says, patting my leg. She rises to walk back into the kitchen.

"How long have you been married?" I ask her and the question came out before I even realized what I said. "I'm sorry, I shouldn't have even asked. Megan told me her grandfather has Alzheimer's."

She turns to me and smiles. Walking over to a picture frame she picks it up and hands it to me and I cannot help but smile. They don't look more than eighteen years old. He is in a military uniform, and she is in a simple, yet lovely, white wedding gown. When I look up at her I notice she has tears in her eyes, "He will forever be the love of my life even if most days he doesn't know who I am." she sighs, "We had a wonderful life together, two beautiful children and then when our grandchildren came along, the world got even better. Sure, we have had some dark days, but the good outweighs them all." I hand her back the picture with a smile and she puts it back on the shelf.

"I dream of that kind of love, someday." I say smiling at her.

"Wait for the man who is your best friend." She grabs my hand and squeezes it. "Now," she says pulling me with her into the kitchen, "Let's eat some lunch."

The screen door flies open. Megan, Collin, and Logan all come busting in the door and grabbing seats around the table.

"Eat up, city girl," Logan looks at me with a clesrly amused with himself, "you got stalls to muck this evening."

I roll my eyes.

Z

Who knew horses could shit so much. I cleaned these stalls yesterday and yet here I am doing it again this evening. I have emptied the wheelbarrow at least five times. I swear I am going to be smelling poop for days. Scooping up another pile and throwing it in the wheelbarrow I look around at the work I've done so far. The stalls are all free of poop and full of fresh shavings and look so much better!

"You're a pro." Megan says, walking down the barn hall with a horse by her side. She stops when she gets to me and ties the horse up to the panels.

"I really think my nose is going to fall off." I say scooping up another pile and putting it in the wheelbarrow.

She laughs and starts undoing the horse's saddle. I put my shovel up against the wall and walk over to the panels looking down at what she's doing.

"Do you have to ride them every day?" I ask her as she takes off the saddle. She sits it down and looks at me.

"The young ones I do." She points at the horse, "This is a colt I'm breaking, and my goal is to start back barrel racing on him someday. He is one of our two-year olds." She turns to pick up her saddle, taking it to the tack room, and I walk out of the stall I am in and walk over to him. His ears prick up and I cannot help but think how beautiful he is. He is a reddish color with light tones and a fire red mane.

She comes walking out, "The young ones keep so much pent-up energy. Riding them every day gets it out, plus it helps get them used to someone on their backs." She pats the colt on the neck. "This here is Crackerjack." She points to another stall, "He's one of that young mare's colts and so far, he's one of my favorites."

I smile at her, "He's beautiful."

I turn from him and walk back over to the stall picking up my shovel and continue working. Megan takes Crackerjack back to his stall, getting the next one out that needs ridden.

I am finishing up laying fresh shavings in the stalls I have cleaned and put the wheelbarrow and shovel up in the tack room. Opening the fridge in the tack room, I take a water and wipe the sweat off of my face. I have seriously never worked so hard in my life.

"Stalls don't look clean enough." Logans voice sounds from the tack room door.

I give him a side eye while drinking my water.

He walks in with a bridle and hangs it up. He looks at me quickly.

"You look like hell." He says turning and walking out of the tack room.

I follow him out but do not say a word. "What? Not going to argue with me?" he smirks.

"I have no energy for annoying people, such as yourself."

He gives me a devilish grin, "I want to show you something, come on." He walks past me and into the side stall of the barn. I'm curious as to what he is going to show me, so I follow him. He disappears behind a sheet of plywood, and I turn to follow him. My eyes widen with happiness when I see what is on the other side.

It's the calf we rescued from the creek, and it is drinking milk from it's mama. Logan stands in front of them with his arms crossed, "It's a little girl." He says to me without looking at me. My heart flutters with happiness and the biggest smile crosses my face.

"Is she going to be okay?" I ask him, bending down closer to the calf.

"Thanks to you, she will." He says bending down with me.

"Thanks Ivy. You did well this morning. Maybe I was wrong about you not being able to pull your weight around here." He smirks at me.

I laugh, "Oh, don't get all mushy with me now, Logan." I roll my eyes playfully.

He eyes turn to something sinful as he looks at me, "I'm a man of many personalities."

I blush and look away from him and back at the calf. He stands and starts walking out of the stall and comes back with fresh hay for bedding.

I stay bent down watching the calf drink milk, mesmerized by the beauty of such a small creature. After a moment, she stops drinking and looks my way.

"Hey, pretty girl." I tell her. "What are we going to call you?" I ask her and her tail swishes. Slowly, she takes a step towards me and sniffs the air near me. Step by step, she slowly gets closer and closer to me until her nose touches my hand.

"Well, I'll be," Logan says standing behind me, "I think she's picked her human."

I smile. "What will we call her?" I ask him.

He's silent for a moment, and then bends down again beside me and the calf, "I think it's only fair that the one who saved her gets to name her." He says but continues looking at the calf.

"So, what name did you pick?" I ask him.

He looks at me, "I didn't save her. You did." I look back at him shocked and confused.

"We would have never known she was there if you hadn't heard her and her mom when you did." He says, looking back at the calf, "You get to pick her name." I smile at him for a moment seeing a side of him I did not realize he had. *Tinder.*

"What do we want to call you?" I ask the young heifer. Her tail wiggles and she spins her heels around running through the stall with zoomies. Logan and I both laugh.

"Let's call you Maggie!" I say to the calf. "Do you like that name?" she walks over to me and nudges my hand.

"I'll take that as a yes!" I smile, happy with the name choice I picked.

"Why Maggie?" Logan asks with an intrigued look on his face.

"Honestly?" I start, "I can't remember where I heard the name when I was a young girl, but I've always thought it was beautiful." I smile, "and she's a beautiful girl."

Logan nods his head, "Just like her human." I blush unsure where that came from but he stands and walks out. I follow slowly behind. We walk out into the barn and Tiny sticks his head out of his stall.

I stop at him and give him a rub on the nose. "You are the best boy, aren't you?" I say to him rubbing his nose again.

"For someone who hasn't grown up around this life. You sure look comfortable around here." Logan says leaning up against Tiny's stall wall.

I shrug my shoulders, "I can't explain it. Once I got up in the saddle and relaxed, it was like my muscles knew what to do."

He cocks an eyebrow, "And you didn't ride horses or anything as a kid?" he asks me.

I sigh, "Not that I'm aware of. My life has been nothing but city life. Prim and proper." I shrug and he nods.

Silence falls over us and Logan just stares at me with Tiny.

In the distance a bell is ringing, and I jump, looking up at Logan. "What the hell is that?" A look of concern crosses my face.

Logan chuckles, "It's supper time." He says walking towards the house, and I follow behind him in silence.

8

I wish I had grown up with a grandmother like Margaret. She is everything I've ever seen in a sweet small town family movie and her cooking is delicious. When we walked into the house, the table was covered with chicken breast, mac and cheese, cream potatoes, green beans and rolls. She had a pitcher of sweet tea sitting in the middle and she was filling up cups of ice.

"Oh my. This looks delicious." I say to her taking a seat beside Megan. Margaret smiles at me and says, "Oh, Ivy dear, there's an envelope for you on the bar." I look at her confused and get up to grab it. Opening it up, I gasp. It's a check for one hundred and fifty dollars from the farm signed by Margaret and an iPhone.

I look up and she smiles, "What? You didn't think I'd let you work for free, did you?" she continues pouring a glass of tea, "Plus, I need a way to be able to contact you if needed."

Megan is smiling at me and says, "You deserve to have something for yourself. Make a clean start."

Tears fill my eyes and I fold the check putting it in my pocket along with the new phone. "I seriously don't know what I'd do without y'all these last few days. This has been so random. But I am entirely grateful." I smile sitting back down at the table.

Logan is staring at me and once our eyes meet, he says, "Ivy, nothing's random, remember?" He smirks, shaking his head at me and we all start putting food on our plates.

Collin comes busting in the door, "Sorry I'm late," he says removing his hat and taking a seat beside logan, "Tractor was giving me problems." He looks exhausted.

"After supper I'll come out and help you with it." Logan says to him.

We all dive into our meals in silence, too hungry to talk. Eventually Megan says, "How's Grandfather today?" asking Margaret.

Margaret doesn't look up from her plate and takes a bite as if she doesn't want to discuss it but finally says, "He was in good spirits today. You guys need to go see him sometime this week. Becky says he's been asking about you." She replies and the conversation stops there.

***

"I wish I had a grandmother like yours when I was growing up." I tell Megan as we wash the dishes after supper together. Collin and Logan went out to work on the tractor and Margaret went to the restaurant to check in on everyone.

She smiles at me, "She's one of kind." She starts to say, "When my parents died, she and my grandfather took us in without a second thought. I was five and Collin was not even two years old, yet." She pauses as if the memory is hard.

"Oh, Megan, I'm so sorry. I had no idea." I say putting my hand on her shoulder. She wipes away a tear and then walks over putting a plate up in the cabinet.

"My uncle and parents were going to a livestock sale. They had a big plan for a cattle and horse breeding farm someday." She starts to say, "but they never made it to the auction." She paused to take a deep breath. "Their truck and trailer was hit head on by an eighteen-wheeler whose driver was driving drunk on a back road. They were confirmed dead on scene. My grandparents tried their hardest to make the breeding program and farm work like their dreams, but grandfather got sick, and it's just been hard," She wipes away a tear and I embrace her in a bear hug.

"I am so sorry." I say to her with tears in my eyes.

"I hate it for Collin. At least I can remember them some, he has no memory of them. Grandma and Grandpa are all he's ever known." She smiles at me, "I'm glad you came into our life, Ivy. I hope you stay around awhile." She squeezes my hand.

The screen door flies open, and we both jump and turn towards it, "Come quick!" Collin screams as he opens the door, "Molly's in labor!" he closes the door as fast as he appeared and runs off.

"Shit," Megan says looking at her phone, "My phones on silent, I never got the foal alert notification."

Grabbing our coats, Megan and I both run out the door where the dogs are standing looking around at all the commotion from the front porch. When we start running towards the barn, they run off with us.

My heart is hammering in my chest as we get close to the barn. "How is she?" Megan asks Collin as we catch up to him and enter the barn.

"She's been pushing only for a few minutes now." Logan says coming out of the tack room with a blanket and some other things I can't really pay attention to because *holy hell, he's shirtless.* His abs are rock solid and my mouth goes dry. He has grease all over his jeans and his baseball cap is backwards on his head. Suddenly the Georgia heat is getting to me. He is full of sweat and grease from the tractor. I gulp as he walks past me.

"This will be a good one for city girl to learn with." My trance is gone immediately at the statement.

"I'm honored." I mumble sarcastically walking around to stare at Molly in her stall and not the half-naked guy who apparently makes me turn into a hormonal teenager.

"She looks so uncomfortable." They all giggle at my naive statement, "Yeah I would be too if I had to push something like that out of me." Collin says and I nod agreeing.

Molly is a natural, you can tell she has obviously done this a time or two. She is laying down on her side in her stall and pushing with each contraction. I ask Megan after a few minutes of watching her if we should intervene and she says, "We don't like to intervene unless absolutely necessary. Once the water breaks, we give her about fifteen to twenty minutes and then intervene if needed. We also want to make sure the baby is positioned nicely."

Suddenly, two front hooves are seen coming through, along with a nose. We all jump up and down with joy. I grab Logan's arm and he jumps like I've startled him, "Sorry," I say putting my hand down, "This is just so exciting." He smiles at me, and we lock eyes for a moment.

"I need to break the sac." Megan states loudly, opening the gate to Molly's stall and snapping me and Logan out of our eye lock.

"Is everything okay?" I ask concerned.

"If I don't help open the sac the baby can't breathe. It just helps it come on out." In one smooth contraction, Molly lets out a big push and the baby comes all the way out. Megan acts quickly and tears open the sac. "Good mama." Megan says to Molly and gets up to walk back to us to let mama finish the job.

I am tearing up and so happy when she walks back to me, "That was the most beautiful thing I've ever seen." I watch the little foal look around and lick its lips. Its sweet little hooves are so small and delicate looking.

"Would you look at that." Collin says, pointing to the foal who has its legs spread open now.

"Oh. My. God!" Megan squeals.

"What's wrong?" I ask confused.

"Nothing's wrong, Ivy! It's a boy! We finally got our stud colt from Molly!" she screams, jumping up and down.

I'm still looking at her confused and she realizes I'm still new here. She smiles, "Molly has never given us a colt. My uncle and parents wanted our stud to come from Molly because of her bloodline and the studs we breed her from." She smiles so big. "This is huge, Ivy! It will help the breeding program take off in a few years!" She's smiling, and I smile big too now that I'm understanding.

"Wow." I say smiling, "Teach me all the ways. I want to help."

"Oh my gosh, are you serious?" she says smiling at me.

I nod and she's hugging me.

"We might turn you into a country girl after all." Logan says to me with a wink and walking into the stall with a towel to rub down the foal. My train of thought is gone again. That wink took my breath away. I turn to watch him with the foal in the stall and my cheeks flush, his back muscles are well-defined and *dear lord get me out of here before im begging him to do things I shouldn't be begging him for.* .

"She already eats like a country girl." Collin says and then his eyes widen like he's realized what he just said out loud. Luckily for him, I was too busy looking at Logan and I didn't fully hear what he was telling me.

"Shit, don't hurt me." he exclaims as if scared, pulling up his two pointer fingers and crossing them as if it's a force field.

Megan busts out laughing, and we all turn back to Molly watching her and the new baby.

9

I've been on the farm for a month now and it's been the best time of my life. I know that is saying a lot considering where I am from, but I finally feel like I am where I was meant to be all along. I have learned how to saddle my own horse and my riding skills have improved. I tend to baby animals, and contrary to Logan's beliefs, I *can* sling bales of hay around. A few foals have been born since the day I arrived, and I have gotten to help with that process. It has been the best therapy for my mental health. I haven't heard from my parents, Courtney, or Stephen and I decided it is for the best. Eventually, I will call my parents and maybe I'll even invite them out to the farm to see what I've been doing. I don't know if I will ever forgive my sister though.

The farm has been the hardest work I've ever done, but also the most rewarding. Molly's newborn colt has grown so much since he was born, and we work with him daily to make sure he's used to be being handled at an early age.

Its mid-morning and Megan and I are sitting at the kitchen table with Margaret running over our breeding program ideas and other plans we have for the farms future. "I agree to all of it." Margaret says and then turns to me, "It's going to be a lot for you to learn. Are you up for that?"

I nod. "I have the feeling this is where I am meant to be." I smile at her and she smiles back.

"I knew there was something about you." She winks at me, "Lets make it final." She states pushing a paper to me.

It's a formal ledger and at the top it stays, "MAGNOLIA FARM BREEDING PARTNERSHIP."

My eyes widen, "W-what?" I say looking back and forth at them both smiling back at me.

"Sweetheart, I'm not a spring chicken anymore." Margaret starts, taking my hand. "Lord willing, I will be here for more years to come, but we never know what the future holds. I can't keep up like I used to and Megan needs someone dependable to help her. Collin still has some growing up to do and Logan can be a little too hard-headed." She looks to Megan and Megan nods.

She looks back at me, "You have been such a big help around here. You will have a lot to learn but I trust you will do just fine. Megan will teach you. I would much rather get this out of the way now, before anything out of our control happens. If something were to happen to me, I at least know Megan will have someone else to help her with the legal side of things." She smiles. "Welcome to the family, Ivy." She pushes the paper towards me.

With tears filling my eyes I pick up the pen she lays beside it with a shaky hand and sign my name on the legal document making Megan and I breeding partners.

"You all are just full of surprises." I grin at both of them.

They both giggle and Megan looks at me with a intrigued look, "Ready for the first adventure *partner*?" she smiles at me, and I cock an eyebrow confused.

"There's a mare across state that I've had a deposit on since before she was born. We paid a deposit for her while she was in the womb. She's now a year old and ready to come home to the farm to eventually be apart of the breeding program."

I smile and nod, waiting for her to explain what that means for me. "One of us needs to go pick her up." She starts, "I can't leave the farm because of the prior arrangements I have with some sales." She looks at me, "But now that we are partners, one of us has to sign to get her here. Think you can handle it?" she asks me confidently.

"Of course!" I say excited, "But wait, I've never driven a trailer before."

"Don't worry, Logan can go with you." She stands, giving her grandmother a hug. I smile to Margaret and thank her.

"I would send Collin but I'm sure you would kill him before you get halfway there." We both laugh at the statement because she's most likely right. We step off the front porch with the dogs on our heels.

"When do I need to be there?" I ask her.

"Tomorrow around lunch. So, you need to leave by tonight. It's a few hours from here." She looks around and turns, seeing Logan throwing hay off the bed of a truck and into the pasture he's parked by. He's shirtless again. *Holy hell.* The way the muscles in his arms are defined as he holds the bale of hay before throwing it over the fence would make any woman tremble at her knees.

"Logan!" she says, and he turns to face us, "Need you to take a trip with Ivy tonight!" she bosses, and he nods. *He needs to put on a damn shirt if he expects me to get in the truck with him.*

***

A little after lunch, I am standing in the yard with the dogs lying next to my feet, with a pillow and an overnight bag on my shoulder. I am watching Logan back the truck up to the gooseneck horse trailer. We are taking the white four-door Chevy that is used most of the time around the farm. I take a deep breath as I watch the truck back to the horse trailer, feeling a little relieved that he is going, and that he is driving. The horse trailer is massive. It fits at least four fully grown horses and has a large living quarter. I would never be able to pull it myself. Megan and Collin went with their grandmother to see their grandfather. Logan and I made sure everyone in the barn was secure in their stalls before we left. Apparently, the farm we are going to is called The Double J Ranch. Logan says he has never been there before, but Megan assured us it was a lovely place.

"Ready?" Logan asks while hooking up the wiring for the taillights to work from the truck to the trailer. I nod and walk up to the truck opening the passenger door, throwing my bag and pillow in the back, and jump into the passenger seat.

A few moments later, Logan pulls open the driver's door and grabs the handle at the top to get in. He must have showered before we left because he's in clean clothes and actually smells nice. His ball cap is turned around backwards, and I have to remind myself not to stare at him.

"What's the address again?" he asks me, and I pull out my phone to the text Megan sent me.

"1564 Kilmanns Road," I pause, searching the rest of the message, "Parkerville, Georgia." I say, dropping my phone in the cup holder. He nods and puts it into the truck's GPS.

Pulling out of the driveway, he has to make the turn wide to get the trailer all of the way out without hitting anything and I think to myself, *yeah, I would not have been able to do that.*

Logan turns the volume on the radio up and Riley Green's song, "Different 'Round

Here" starts to play and I watch as the town comes into our sight. The song fits it perfectly. This town almost makes me feel like it is a town the world has forgotten. It's a whole other world compared to what I have grown up in. The fields with farmhouses and people waving as we go by is something that makes my heart flutter with joy. So many places have gotten away from the simple things.

I'm broken out of the trance of my surroundings when I hear Logan singing beside me. I turn my head and beam, "Whoa, country boy can sing." I grin at him, and he laughs.

"Nah, just love that song. It reminds me to be thankful where I'm from." He turns on his blinker as the GPS tells us to get on the interstate. The same interstate I came here on. I chuckle under my breath at the thought of how much my life has changed in just a month.

While Logan is merging on the interstate, I grab the auxiliary cord for the radio and he looks at me, "Oh no. No one touches my radio other than me." he says grabbing it out of my hand. I grab it back from him and smile, "You will just have to get over it." I smirk pulling the auxiliary cord from him, "Just drive and let me worry about the tunes." I say, connecting my phone to the cord and searching my phone for what I'm in the mood for. I decide to put on 90's Country music and sit my phone back down in the cup holder.

"Write this down" by George Strait comes on and I start singing along. Logan shoots me a look, "Well I'll be," he says laughing, "Never pegged you for a country music girl."

I laugh, "There is many things you most likely get wrong about me." I smile and pull my legs up into the seat and lean back and get comfortable. I ignore his stare and start singing again.

"Let's get off here, stretch our legs, get some gas and eat." Logan says a couple hours later. I nod. It's now dark out and we need to be finding somewhere to sleep soon. We have made our way into South Georgia but still have at least an hour to go in the trip.

Logan turns off on exit four and my eyes catch a Zax sign. "Oh!" I holler, "Let's go get some Zax!" I say turning to Logan. He makes a disgusted face and I fly my hands over my mouth in a dramatic gasp.

"Don't tell me you are against the greatest chicken place ever." I say shocked.

"It's okay," he starts, "Just not my cup of tea."

I laugh, "Well what is your cup of tea?" I ask him.

He looks at me with eyes that twinkle and for a moment my heart stops. His eyes go from mine, to my lips, my body, and then back up to my eyes. We are stopped at a red light, but his eyes don't leave mine. He looks like he's in deep thought and then he looks away as the light turns green, "Zax is fine, Ivy." He says with a snarl and then turns towards its direction. I'm now feeling uneasy. Did we just have a moment? *What the hell was that reaction* I think to myself.

We park in the back parking lot and take up about six parking spaces with the truck and trailer eventually making our way inside. It's empty other than a few people sitting in the booths eating. There's no line at the front to order so we both walk up and the girl standing at the computer looks at us. Correction, she looks *at Logan*. I roll my eyes. He doesn't even notice her staring. I stare a hole in her until she looks at me and then back down at the computer like she has been caught. Why am I jealous? Logan and I aren't even a couple or *anything*. We just work together. Stop acting like a jealous girlfriend.

"Welcome." The girl finally says, "What can I get for you?" she asks but starts staring at Logan again with a flirtatious smile on her face.

"Umm," Logan says looking at the menu behind her on the wall, "Grab me the number three please, extra pickles, water to drink." He turns to me, "And whatever my girlfriend wants." My heart skips a beat.

Girlfriend?

The girl stutters as if the words he just spoke broke her heart, "Oh," she turns to me, "What can I get you, miss?" she gives me a small fake smile.

"Umm, same thing as him," I grin at her. Logan reaches in his wallet and takes out the farm credit card to pay with. The girl hands us our drinks and Logan wraps his arm around my waist out of nowhere, walking us to the drink counter. My heart is doing all kinds of flips.

After filling our cups, I walk around picking a booth for us to sit at. "What the hell was that?" I ask him as we both sit.

He looks at me, "What?"

"You know exactly what." I say pointing my finger at him.

He takes a sip of his drink, his eyes never leaving mine, and he leans forward. "I just didn't want her flirting with me." he says with a shrug of his shoulders.

I laugh, "You got a girlfriend or something?" I ask him, halfway wanting him to say no now that I've asked.

"No, Ivy. I'm single." He pauses, "I had a serious girlfriend at one point a few years ago. After my parents died, we both went our separate ways." He states, but he doesn't grin or smile. He just stares at me this time. There's an unspoken something about what his eyes are saying. I can feel my face blush.

We eat our food in silence mostly because we were both starving. Once we are done, Logan takes our trays and throws all of our trash away and we refill our cups for the road.

Pulling myself up in the truck, Logan turns on the engine and is typing another destination into the GPS. *Destination in 5 miles.* The GPS says after he pulls out onto the main road.

My head snaps to his, "Where are we going?" I ask him as he turns into the gas station to fill up the truck.

"We need sleep, Ivy. Plus, we aren't scheduled to be there until morning." He says opening his door. He jumps out and turns to me, "Megan rented us a room for the night at a Hilton down the road." He closes his door and walks to the pump.

I slide back in my seat pulling my knees up to my chest.

I sure the hell hope she got two separate rooms or at least two beds.

10

"Reservation for Logan Parker." Logan says to the woman as we walk up to the check in desk. She's an older woman who resembles a librarian with her glasses hanging on the end of her nose and her silver hair pulled on top of her head. Patsy is the name on her name tag, and I smile at the uniqueness of it. She types on her computer, not looking at us, and then states, "I need a debit or credit card on file."

Logan takes out his wallet and hands her the farm credit card. She scans it and hands it back to him swiftly. A printer turns on and starts working, she grabs the papers and staples them together.

"Here is your receipt," she says handing the papers him. "Take the elevator to the right that's around the corner and you're on the fourth floor, room number four-fifteen." We nod and thank her. She turns back to the computer, not caring anymore about us.

Logan is looking at the receipt when we make it to the elevator, so I press the button for us. The doors open immediately, and we step inside. Logan is still running over the receipt as if he's confused.

The door closes and I press the button for the fourth floor then I turn to him, "Everything okay?" I ask him.

He puts the papers down suddenly and doesn't look at me, "Yes everything is great. Sorry, just checking to make sure she didn't over charge us." I cock my eyebrow at him but stay silent.

The elevator doors open and we step out looking at how the rooms are numbered down the hall. We turn right down the straight hall and walk until we see our room number. Logan puts the room key into the door and it flashes green for us to open. Turning the handle and opening the door, Logan lets me walk in first. First thing I notice is the bathroom is on the left, with a nice walk-in shower, large sink area and toilet. Farther down is a little kitchenette, and then I freeze.

"What the hell, Megan." I say out loud, and I hear Logan coming up behind me.

"Yeah," he starts to say, running his hands through his hair and sitting his bag down on the floor by the tv and dresser. "That's what I noticed in the receipt." He walks over to the window and opens the blinds. The lights outside from businesses and restaurants light up the world below.

There is only one bed in this room, granted it is king-sized, but still only one.

"I'll sleep on the floor, Ivy. It's no big deal." He says to me walking back from the window and grabbing the tv remote off the nightstand.

I stand in silence as he turns the tv on and sits on the end of the bed. He goes through the channels for a bit and we don't say a word.

"N-No," I say to him trying to find my words, "We are adults, it's okay. At least it's a king bed." I shrug and walk over to grab my bag off the floor. "I am going to change into some pajamas. I'm exhausted." He nods and continues flipping through the channels.

I throw my bag on the bathroom counter and rub my hands over my face in exhaustion. *Stop being dramatic,* I tell myself, *you are an adult. You can handle this as such.* I reach for the zipper on my bag and open it up and grab a pair of shorts Megan let me borrow and a t-shirt I recently bought from one of the stores in town. Unclasping my bra, I pull it off and stuff it in my bag, so he doesn't have to see it. I run a brush through my hair and grab my toothbrush and toothpaste out of my bag and brush my teeth.

Once I rinse my teeth with water, I leave my toothbrush on the counter for in the morning and open the door to walk out. I can hear the sound of the television on, and I sit my bag down on the floor outside the bathroom. Looking up and stopping in my tracks, I gasp. Logan is laying on top of the covers, with his back up against the headboard, shirtless, and in grey sweatpants.

"That's what you sleep in?" I ask with my eyes trying not to stare at his perfect abs. He laughs taking his eyes off the tv and looking at me, "Is that a problem?" he smirks, cocking an eyebrow. I swear he is flirting with me. I shake my head no and walk over to the bed.

My hands pull back the covers and I sit down slowly, pulling the covers up over my legs and lean back with my head on the pillow. Suddenly, my exhaustion is gone and I'm energetic after seeing him like that. He has my blood pumping in places it shouldn't be. "What are you watching?" I ask, trying to not be so awkward.

He grabs the remote and sits it down near me, "Nothing good was on so I just clicked on the cartoon channel." I giggle and he smirks, "Okay, honestly, I like cartoons. I'm a big kid."

He says pulling the covers back and getting under them. My body stiffens as I feel the warmth of his body near mine.

We lay in silence watching Tom and Jerry cartoons for a little while laughing and giggling at the tv. Not once do we look at each other or make eye contact and I have a feeling he's as tense as I am.

For a brief moment, I feel his foot rub mine and I pull my foot back almost instantly.

"Oh, I didn't mean to." He said to me as soon as it happened. "I had an itch." He looks at me and I look back at him. we stare at each other like we both can see into each other's soul. I can tell he's debating on telling me something.

Logan sits up using his arm to hold his head up and he lets out a big breath then ask, "Ivy, can I be honest about something?" my heart does a little flip and I nod.

He sighs, "I don't know." he rubs his hand throw his hair and looks away and then back to me trying to read my face, "I don't know what your ex was thinking when he did you the way he did." His eyes darken and butterflies enter my stomach. My lips part slowly as if I'm shocked at the words I am hearing.

He goes on, "I mean, if you were mine, I wouldn't go a day without showing you how treasured you are. I wouldn't even think about another woman." He sighs, "I mean hell, we aren't even together like that, and I can't get you off my mind." There's so much passion in his voice, I can feel my body warm up again. "I'd worship the ground you walked on. I'd show you how a woman is supposed to be treated." He looks away as if embarrassed at what he just said. Then he suddenly looks back at me sinfully, "I had you wrong all along. It's because of the moment I saw you out there on the dance floor, I felt pulled to you. The moment Megan told me you were coming to work with us, I knew I was a goner." He said and I haven't realized the entire time that he's closer to me now.

I smile at him, placing my hand on his chest, "You are only saying that because I have no bra on, and we are in the same bed together."

He puts his forehead on mine as if he's thinking and then looks at me, "I have wanted you since the moment you poured that beer on me." he says with a smile. And to prove it to you, I won't try a single thing tonight." He wraps his arms around my waist and turns me around to place us in a spooning position.

Well, this just took a turn I was not expecting.

But it's a nice feeling being held by someone. I reach up and turn the lamp light off and snuggle back into him. He is snoring. I smile and close my eyes.

Sweet dreams, Logan.

***

I feel the bed dip beside me, and I slowly stir awake. Sluggishly opening my eyes, I see Logan walking into the bathroom. It wasn't a dream. Logan Parker confessed his feelings for me last night. Wait, I look around and notice it's still dark outside. I look at the clock on the nightstand and its only two o clock in the morning. I lay my head back down and try to go back to sleep when I hear the toilet flush and the bathroom door open.

His footsteps are walking along the bed to his side and he dips back into the bed puling the covers over him. I struggle with the option of going back to sleep or letting him know I'm awake too.

"I thought I was dreaming." I say turning to him.

He smiles at me and brushes the hair out of my face, "What do you mean?"

I lean up and touch his abs trailing my fingers back and forth over the creases, "I thought I dreamed I went to sleep snuggled up to you." I smile and inch closer to him rubbing my hand over his chest more intensely.

"Are you sad it was real?" he asks, cocking an eyebrow at me.

I shake my head no. He lifts my chin to stare into my eyes for a brief moment. With one quick move, he grabs my hips and pulls me over him where I'm straddling him. The covers pooled all around us.

I bend down to his ear and whisper, "What did you mean a while back when you said you had many personalities?" I face him and his adams apple moves slowly.

"Are you sure you want to know?" he asks me while he's eyeing my lips.

I nod and within one full move, his lips are on mine. He turns me over so my back is now on the mattress. His tongue slides out parting my lips and I follow his move. He pulls back from me, "You tell me to stop, and I'll stop immediately." He says to me, and I nod, crashing my lips back to his. A growl comes out of his body and he's pulling away, making his way down my stomach pulling my shorts down while trailing kisses as he goes. My panties are the only thing keeping us separate now.

I gasp. I haven't been touched like this in a long time, if ever. Stephen was not the intimate type. He was worried about his pleasure and his pleasure only. It wasn't about me or touching me.

Logan lifts the bottom of my t-shirt up and I keep my eye on his. They blacken. His breathing deepens when he notices my breasts are free under my shirt. He pulls me to him and takes one nipple into his mouth. It hardens instantly at the tug. He does the same to the other nipple. I can feel my panties getting more wet by the minute. Our breathing becomes frantic and he turns me around where my back is on the bed and he's leaning over me.

Slowly making his way down my body he spills kisses all over my stomach and hips. Suddenly, his teeth take the top of my panties in his mouth, and he tugs them down slowly. His eyes never leave mine.

This man is full on alpha male.

"No fair." I say breathlessly to him as he pulls my panties off completely and tosses them behind him on the floor.

He smiles up at me, "What's not fair." He lowers himself back down to where my panties use to lay on my hips, and he kisses all around being careful to not hit the spot I need him to.

"I'm completely naked and you are only half." I say in between breaths.

"This is not about my pleasure, Ivy. My only goal right now is showing you how your body is supposed to be worshipped." And as soon as that sentence leaves his mouth, his mouth is on me. Making his way down my body slowly. He kisses my stomach, my hips, and my belly button. Then, his tongue runs down the entrance of the spot I have been wanting him to take. He trails his tongue over my clit and then he's sucking with so much power it makes my back arch. This is a first for me. No one has ever cared enough about me for my pleasure to be the only thing on their mind. I am overwhelmed by emotions. I feel his tongue back on me now and I hear the rustle of the sheets. One finger enters me as he goes back to sucking on my clit and another finger slides in within a few seconds. I can feel him stretching me.

Another finger goes in, and he curls them just enough to hit my g-spot. My body is experiencing all forms of overwhelming pleasure like I have never experienced before. He looks up at me and his eyes are dark with something primal. *Holy shit*. He's turned on just by watching me. He continues fingering me and runs his tongue over my clit that is now so sensitive from all his sucking. His tongue gets erotic, and I feel my body tense and my pussy clamps down around his fingers. My back arches off the bed and my toes curl, but he doesn't stop the rhythm. If anything, he intensifies it. I let out a loud moan. Another one comes up behind, and then another and my toes curl again and my back arches again. AND Again – OH MY GOD!.

He removes his fingers and slowly starts kissing me until he gets to my lips and kisses me even harder than before. I can taste my cum on his lips and I suddenly have an urge to please him the way he has just pleased me, even though I have never wanted to do it before.

I push him down on the bed and start kissing him down to his stomach but when I get to his sweatpants, he stops me. I am being pulled back up to him as he kisses me softly. I know he needs a release. I can see the massive bulge in his pants.

"Not tonight." He tells me and pulls me into his arms, cuddling and wrapping covers around us.

I'm confused, "W-why not?"

He kisses me on the side of the head and nestles beside me, "Because that was about you, not me." he pauses, "I told you I have many personalities. Now let's get a few more hours of sleep." He tells me, and I smile with tears in my eyes full of respect for this *MAN*.

Sweet dreams, my grumpy cowboy.

11

That was the best sleep ever. If orgasms are supposed to feel like that, then I have never had one in my life.

The sun is just now coming up when I roll over and smile at the beautiful human lying beside me. I remember the first night I met him and how we did not start off on the right foot. He is softer than most people get to see from him. I run my hands over his chin back up to his ear and he stirs.

"Good morning, beautiful." Logan says opening his eyes and trying his best to wake up.

Smiling at him I run my hands over his chest, "Did I dream I had the best orgasm of my life last night?"

He does a soft laugh and rolls me over, so my back is lying flat on the bed and he's hovering over me.

"The best?" he smirks and leans down to kiss me on the neck and my breast, teasing me as he flips his tongue over my nipples that seem to harden at that exact moment.

"Uh huh," I reply losing my train of thought. He laughs and comes back up to me smiling and kissing me softly on the lips.

"As much as I want to give you more, looking at how beautiful you are this morning," he kisses me on the lips, "we need to hit the road." And I frown at him.

"Oh shit!" I say, grabbing my phone seeing I had a few missed texts from Megan, "What are we going to tell her and Collin?"

Logan gets off the bed and stretches his arms above his head and laughs at me, "I'm pretty sure Megan had this planned all along, seeing as she only booked us a one bed." He walks into the bathroom, and I hear the shower turn on.

Smiling like an idiot, I lay back on the headboard with my phone. Opening my messages I read over my unread text from Megan.

Oh, meant to warn you, I only booked a one-bedroom room. Hope that is okay.

Send me pics soon as you get her loaded. All you have to do is sign the papers. We will send them a check in the mail. Any issues just call me.

P.S. Hope you had a good night sleep. ;)

I hit call and hope Logan stays in the shower until I'm done talking to her.

"Hello?" Megan says on the other line.

"You sneaky Bitch!" I hear her giggle in the background, and I let out a sigh.

"Did my plan work?" she asks proud of herself.

"I'd say the two orgasms I had last night would say yes." I laugh putting my hand on my forehead shaking it.

"OH MY GOD!" I hear Megan squealing. "I knew he was into you!" I can literally hear her jumping up and down.

"How the hell did I not notice?" I ask her sternly.

And within that second, I can't hear a single word she's saying because Logan comes walking out of the bathroom, fully naked, dripping wet, and walks over to me. I gulp. He's huge. I mean, I could tell by his bulge last night, but *DAMN.* My breathing stops. He grabs the phone out of my hand and puts it to his ear, "Megan?" he says on the other end, "I need Ivy. I'll let her call you back later." All I hear is squeals on the other end. He hangs up and throws my phone on the bed. In one quick move, I'm being picked up and carried into the shower with him.

"Logan!" I squeal playfully as he puts me down under the water, removing my shirt that I had on.

He smirks and my hair is now officially all wet, but I don't care. His little boyish smile is something I could never get enough of. He leans into me and trails kisses all down my neck, my shoulders, and runs his hands over my hips.

"I was just standing in here but all I could think about is you." He kisses my lips and I smile into it. "Sorry for getting your hair wet." He says shrugging.

I wrap my arms around him and kiss him harder than the soft kisses he was giving me before. Breaking away from our kiss, he takes the shampoo the hotel puts in the rooms and lathers it up to wash my hair. I let him. He's careful and caring as he washes my hair and then my body. This is more intimate than the orgasms. It feels like passion. Once he is done, I do the same to him, minus the conditioner for his hair.

Stephen never did this for me, nor did he ever offer. Come to think of it, I never saw my parents or heard them talk about doing sweet things like this for each other either. I was not aware men like this existed.

"Where did you learn to be so sweet?" I ask him as I run the rag I was using to wash his body, over his abs.

It seems like the question I asked pains him, "I watched my parents care for each other for as long as I could remember." He pauses. "I can remember before my mother got sick, she would tell me stories about how my father was to her. And then when she got sick, I can remember watching him care for her." He sighs and puts his hands on mine stopping them and I look up at his eyes, they look sad. "I can remember my mother being so sick, she couldn't eat or drink by herself. My dad would feed her."

Tears prick my eyes and I lean my chest into his, we just stand there under the shower head for what seems like forever.

Eventually I ask, "What kind of sickness did she have?"

I feel him take a deep breath and he answers, "Breast cancer. She was in remission once, but it came back with a vengeance. It took her from us. My dad grieved himself to death shortly after."

I stay silent and just hold on to him. He finally kisses me on the head and says, "I'm glad I met you, Ivy. My parents would have loved you." I smile up at him and he kisses me deeply.

***

It took me about twenty minutes to dry my hair and get ready after our shower, but we were back in the truck before eight and heading to our destination.

Logan has held my hand since we got in the truck. We have passed so many beautiful farms this morning. Pastures full of cows and horses. I don't know how I ever went without knowing this type of life existed. We pull into the driveway of Double J Ranch. I'm overwhelmed with how beautiful the place is. They obviously have money. Logan pulls up to the large iron gate and there's a security guard out front that steps out of his area, "Can I help you?" he asks, eyeing us.

"We are supposed to be picking up a mare we had purchased. Logan Parker." Logan tells him.

The guard walks over to where he came from and pulls out a list on a clipboard. He scans over it more than once.

"I'm sorry," he says looking up and back at the paper. "There's no Logan Parker on my paper. I can't let you in."

I bend my head down to where he can see me, "Can you try Ivy Price?" I ask him, "I'm technically the one who will be signing for her." I smile at him, and he looks back at his list.

"Yes, Miss Price, I have you listed." He smiles at me and hits the button for the gate to open. "Once you get up to the fork, take the right, it will lead you to the sale barn. Ask for Ry." He says and turns, walking back to his sitting area. Logan thanks him and rolls up his window.

He grabs my hand again and drives down the driveway. I couldn't be happier even if I tried. I really think I can make this new life work to my benefit.

I look out at the pastures before us and take it all in. This place is a dream of every cowgirl's vision. It's full of horses from all ages and the trees are perfectly placed down the driveway lining it. Once we take the right to the sale barn, I see people out working in arenas, landscapers, and little kids in round pens taking lessons. It looks like a place that our farm could be someday.

Logan pulls the truck and trailer to the side of the barn and we get out looking for someone who could help us. The barn is massive and full of horses in every stall. Everyone seems to be out in the arenas or working. Thankfully we walk up to a blonde whose back is turned to us and talking to a young teenage girl about her riding, possibly from a lesson she had just given. The girl finally nods and walks away leading her horse into a stall. The blondes back is still turned to us as we get closer to her. She's in riding jeans and boots, and I make a mental note that I wish my ass looked that good in jeans. Honestly, she's a perfect mixture of Megan and I. You can tell she's got muscles from years of riding horses and working on a farm.

She turns around and her face goes pale when she's sees us. She honestly looks like she's going to be sick.

"Hey!" I say trying to keep her focus on not throwing up, "My name is Ivy, and this is Lo-"

"Logan!!" the blonde says, throwing herself around him and hugging him so hard I think she might break his neck.

Before I can ask what is going on, she kisses him. A full-on mouth to mouth kiss. I notice he doesn't kiss back and he's as shocked as I am but I'm not sure it's for the same reason.

The blonde lets herself down and looks at him, "What are you doing here?" she asks confused but smiling big.

"We are here to pick up a mare for our farm." I say to her. Realizing how jealous I sound saying *ours*. Shit, am I jealous?

She looks back and forth at me and him and then looks at me sternly, "Who the fuck are you?"

I'm a little taken back from her use of words. It ignites a fire in me, and I take a step towards her, "Better question, who the fuck are you?" I ask her and look sternly at Logan who looks like he wants to be anywhere else right now.

The blonde laughs and by the way it sounds, I'm worried about what she is going to say next. "I'm his fiancé." She says to me and my heart drops. Now I'm the one who is going to puke.

I turn to Logan and his eyes are wide.

"Typical," I whisper, "'So, you lied when you told me you were single?" My eyes are staring into his and I feel a level of hurt I haven't felt since finding Stephen with my sister.

"Single?" Rylee huffs, "Now we know that is not true." She smiles at him flirtatiously.

"Ivy," he starts stepping towards me and I take a step back, he takes the hint and stops but continues, "This is Rylee. She was my girlfriend in high school, and she *was* my fiancé, but when my mother died, I called it off." I watch him snap a side eye at her and she huffs, walking over to him and grabbing the front of his shirt.

"That's not exactly what you said." She turns to me, "He told me we could see other people but eventually we would be back together and get married one day."

Logan turns to her and snaps, "I never said I was coming back for you. I ended our relationship because you are a crazy bitch who wanted to control me all the time." He looks back at me, "Ivy, I promise. I didn't even know she worked here."

She laughs, "Work here? I own it, Logan." She gestures around to the place.

His eyes widen, "You did all of this?" he asks her, sounding interested. She smiles at him, and I really think I might puke.

After a moment, I turn to her, "You know, now that I think about it, we wont be taking the mare today. I would like a refund check, immediately." I say, smiling at Rylee. She turns quickly on her heels and her smile is gone.

"What?" she says almost desperately.

"You heard me," I say, "Keep your mare and refund me. I want nothing to do with your place if this is how you talk to a customer." I say walking closer to her.

She steps back and I can see the desperation in her eyes. She needs our money. Every sale keeps her afloat. "But you can't."

I smile, I can be a bitch, too. "I haven't signed a single thing which means the money that was given to you was just a deposit for when I picked her up. Once I signed for her, the rest would be mailed to you because it would be a legal contract." I point a finger and demand, "Give me a refund and we will be on our way." I look at Logan, "No, actually if you need a new farm hand, keep him." I pause, "I'll be at the truck until I have a check or cash in my hand." I turn on my heels and walk out of the barn.

When I get to the truck, I'm holding my chest trying to catch my breath. What have I done, what was I thinking. Men aren't really loyal, and they don't care about us. Logan didn't follow me to the truck, he stayed behind.

He clearly made his choice. Megan is going to be pissed at me for coming back without this mare, but I think I'm making a smart business decision. I need to start thinking of a plan B and quick.

Fifteen minutes later, Logan walks out of the barn and Rylee is a little behind him. His face is stern and his eyes have not left mine. I straighten up and wipe my eye where a small tear is sitting.

"Ivy, Wait." Logan says reaching where I'm standing. "We need to talk." He says, eyeing me nervously.

"Here." Rylee says handing me a check. "I'm sorry for any miscommunication we may have had between us." She gives me a smile and turns to Logan, "I hope you made the right choice." She walks away from us.

I eye him and cock an eyebrow. He grabs my hand, but I pull it back.

Logan sighs, "Let's talk about this, please, Ivy." He says with pleading eyes.

I shake my head no, "I can't do this with you. I can't be the girl my sister was. I need to figure my shit out first." I open the door of the truck and climb inside shutting the door before he has a chance to reply. He walks around the driver side of the truck slowly and climbs inside. We ride in silence towards the gate.

12

This was the worst idea. I'm coming home with a refund check. No mare. Don't worry, I have a plan.

I shoot the text to Megan as we get on the main road. I'm not sure if I'm more disappointed or mad. I really thought Logan was going to be a guy I could care for, and he would prove me wrong about all men. But I was wrong. The only good thing that came out of this trip was the idea it gave me that I need to run by Megan.

My phone dings almost instantly.

This is something you need to discuss with your partner before making a decision.

I sigh, I knew she wouldn't take it well, but I think my plan will help smooth it over.

Trust me. Please. Will talk to you about it when I get back. On the interstate now.

I know she is most likely going to be pissed at me, but once she hears the reasoning I have, I think she will be happy.

Be safe. I'll have an open mind.
P.S. anymore orgasms?

I sit my phone down and decide it's better to not reply and just talk to her face to face. She's going to want all the details anyways.

I look over and notice the veins sticking out of Logan's forearm. His eyes are glued to the road, and he has a death grip on the steering wheel. I grab the auxiliary chord and plug it into my phone as I scroll through the songs and finally decide to put it on shuffle. Grabbing my pillow from the backseat, I decide a nap would do me some good.

We can deal with this when we get back to the farm.

***

Other than a few stops to use the bathroom and grab something to eat, Logan and I haven't said more than five sentences to each other this whole ride back. I have slept most of the ride and I think it's for the best because if I talk to him about anything right now, I think I might bust out in tears. I'm still fragile and he should know that.

We are finally back in Maple and turning onto the road the farm is on. I haven't been awake long, and my eyes are still trying to adjust to being awake. Its dark outside and the porch light is on for us but I'm sure everyone else has gone to bed. It is late and it looks like everyone in the barn is put up for the night, too. Logan parks and I get out from the truck with my bag as he unhooks the trailer.

I shut the truck door and walk towards the house, "Ivy," Logan says, walking around the truck where I can see him, "Can we talk, please?" he asks me with sad eyes.

I sigh. "Logan, I don't have the energy." I turn halfway to the house then back to him, "Let me think on it tonight. We can talk tomorrow." I say, walking toward the porch.

I hadn't quite made it to the front step when the dogs speed off the porch barking and heading to the barn wide open. In that moment, I hear a howl and it sounds close. I drop my bag with a thud on the ground and look at Logan with wide eyes.

I take off running towards the barn and Logan is not far behind me. We enter the barn and the dogs are running off into the pasture. I look over in Molly's stall and she's gone, so is the baby. Her door has been left wide open. Adrenaline courses through my body.

I turn quickly to Logan and he's thinking the same thing as me. Running to Tiny's stall, I grab his halter and bring him out to the tack area. Logan does the same to the mare that he rode the day we were on the hill. I hear a ring as he puts his phone on speaker, "H-he-hello?" a raspy voice on the other end says and I immediately know it's Megan's.

I run in the tack room and grab the saddle I normally use, and Logan throws his over his mares back.

"Meg, quick, wake Collin." Logan yells while he helps me with my saddle, "Molly is not in her stall. She's let herself out again. Baby is gone, too." I hurry into the tack room and grab our bridles.

"Oh, God." I hear her jump out of bed and run banging on Collin's door.

"There's coyotes in the pasture, dogs have went after them. Bring the guns." We put our bridles on the horses, "Ivy and I are already saddled and heading out. Hurry!!"

We both mount our horses.

Megan yells, "Be careful! We are coming!" The line disconnects.

"I know you hate me right now. But we have to work together." Logan says to me handing me my rope to drape around my horn and gloves. I nod agreeing.

"Let's go." I say and kick Tiny in the sides. We both take off into the pasture at almost a run towards the dogs.

We ride up a hill and I can't see much in front of me because it's so dark. Logan and I forgot to grab flashlights when we ran out of the barn. I trust Tiny to step in the places he needs to step and not fall. This is his home, too. He knows this land better than we do. I can hear water rushing up ahead and I realize where we are, the creek we saved Maggie in just a few weeks ago.

I see an outline of something laying on the ground and I steer Tiny towards it. My heart rate picks up as I realize its Molly and she's hurt.

"Logan!" I scream and he guides his way over to me. Getting down from my saddle I walk over to Molly placing my hands on her neck. I pull out my phone and turn the light on from it. She's not moving much that I can tell but her front foot is hurt from what I can see.

"Where's the baby?" Logan says shining his light from his phone around Molly. I can hear the dogs off in the distance and I look up at Logan with fear. His eyes tell me he fears the same thing.

In that moment, we hear hoof beats and see lights coming up the mountain. Megan and Collin appear as they top the hill.

"Front legs hurt." I tell them as they get close. "But the baby is gone. We don't know where he is." I instantly get a feeling in my gut. If this doesn't go well, everything I did today is for nothing. We have to find him.

I throw a leg over Tiny and look at Megan, "I'm going to follow the dogs trail, they are onto something." Megan nods and hands Logan the pistol that is strapped to her side.

"Collin and I will take care of Molly. You guys go find her baby." Megan says and dismounts her horse. She walks over to Molly laying on the ground. I notice she wipes a tear as she lays her hand on her beloved mare. My heart is breaking for Megan, but we have to find her baby.

I look at Logan, "Ready?" he nods and takes an extra flashlight from Collin. The dogs are getting louder as we head off in their direction.

We get up to the creek where the calf had been rescued a few weeks ago and stopped to listen. Reba has something cornered around the pasture line to our right. We kick the horses into gear straight to her. I let out a breath, thankful we are not going to have to pull anything out of that creek tonight.

Logan shines the flashlight around the fence line. He stops right when he sees Reba. She is standing in front of something, and we stop abruptly when we realize she has put herself in between the colt and a coyote. The coyote is angry and snarling at Reba, but she doesn't let the colt get out from behind her. She is standing her ground and doing her job, protecting the livestock. Izzy and George are right next to her, but they do not look as confident as Reba. She is definitely the alpha.

Logan unclips the pistol from his side and raises it then lowers it again, "I can't get a good shot. I risk hitting the colt or one of the dogs." He says frustrated. I look around and then down at my saddle. "Any ideas?" he asks me, and I give him a look of, *you are not going to like this.*

"One, but you aren't going to like it." He looks at me and at the same time I turn Tiny and start walking around where the coyote could have a better chance at getting to me than the colt. Maybe he would change directions and allow Logan to get a shot.

"Ivy, don't!" Logan starts but I'm already heading in the direction I need to go in.

I hear him take a deep breath and stay where he is. I'm being the diversion. If I can get the coyote's focus off of the dogs and colt, maybe he will get away from them enough for Logan to have a shot. Tiny knows exactly what I'm doing as he prances under me ready to sacrifice himself with me.

I pat his neck, "It's just you and me boy. We are a team." His ears shoot forward and he nods his head. I smile. These animals are magnificent. We walk just a few feet away from Logan but leave enough space from the coyote to give us time to getaway, if needed.

After a few seconds, the coyote turns and looks at me. Reba never makes a move, and the coyote realizes his better chance is coming after me. He takes off towards me in a full stride. I kick Tiny in the sides with my heels and he starts to open his stride too. I hope Logan can get a shot. It's gaining on us and I'm afraid for a moment I've made the worst decision.

BANG.

The sound rings my ears. Tiny jumps and I settle him to slow down as he does a little kick and prance. I look behind me and the coyote is laying on the ground, dead. My heart rate picks up again, and tears fill my eyes. *We did it.*

Tiny and I walk back over to Logan with the dogs and Molly's colt. I dismount Tiny and run up to the dogs, giving them big hugs and telling them what an excellent job they did. Reba's tail is wagging uncontrollably and she is giving me kisses.

"Colt is perfectly healthy." Logan says, standing up from him looking relieved and looking over me checking to make sure I'm not hurt. I shudder at his touch.

"I'm okay." I say pulling back from him.

He sighs, "I'm sorry about everything." He pauses, "Can we talk about it?" he asks with hopeful eyes.

I walk away from him and grab my rope off my horn handing it to him to wrap around the colt's neck to bring him back home.

"Maybe tomorrow." I say, turning to mount Tiny. "I need sleep tonight."

We ride back in silence and I bend down to pat Tiny on the neck and thank him for taking care of us. The dogs run in front of us, leading the way home. For some strange reason, I get a sense of déjà vu, yet again.

It has to be sleep deprivation seeping in.

13

It's well into mid-morning before I roll over in the bed. Once we got back to the barn last night, I helped Megan make sure Molly's stall was locked before leaving them and heading inside. Megan does not think her foot is broken, just sprained, and it can be healed with therapy and injections a few times a week. We got extremely lucky. Once the adrenaline faded last night, I don't remember anything else besides my head hitting the pillow.

I grab my phone and my eyes widen as I realize it's almost lunch time. I've missed chores. My alarm didn't wake me up, someone turned it off and no one woke me up.

I jump out of bed and change clothes quickly. Running into the bathroom, I brush my teeth, my hair, and put on some deodorant. I really need a shower since the last time I showered was with Logan, but I feel bad enough about missing chores and not being there to help.

Running down the stairs two at a time I halt in my tracks as I see Margaret sitting at the kitchen table writing in her book. She wipes a tear from her eye, and I am hesitant to say anything or keep her from what she is doing. I reach down and grab my boots to put them on where they stay by the front door and she looks up, closing her book. "Oh, good morning sweetheart." She says as she stands and puts her book up in a drawer.

I smile as I put my second boot on, "I am so sorry if I interrupted." I tell her apologetically.

She smiles and turns to fix me a glass of orange juice and hands me a jelly biscuit left over my breakfast she had sitting on the table. I smile and take them from her.

"You are never interrupting me." she said. "Sit." She gestures to the seat at the table. I look at her confused, but I know better than to argue with her.

"Logan told me about last night." She pauses as I take a bite of my biscuit, "I think I'll sleep through anything now days. You kids have it all under control." She says to me with a smile.

I give her a smile back, "I'm glad Molly and the colt are going to be just fine…" I say but not so sure where this is going.

"So," she says after a moment, "Megan said you didn't bring the new addition home last night. Instead, you had them give you a refund." I take a big gulp of my orange juice nervously.

"Ivy, I'm not mad." She smiles, "I trust you. I wouldn't have made you and Megan partners if I didn't. Tell me the whole story." She tells me with a smile, and I let a big breath out of my lungs.

This woman is so easy to talk to. She listened to me tell her the whole story, minus the extravagant details of me and Logan, although I did tell her that he did kiss me. She did not seem shocked at all. I told her about Rylee, his ex, or *fiancé*, or whoever she is to him, and how she talked to me. Then I told her the biggest part…My plan.

She listened and she smiled. She didn't argue or try to talk me out of it. She nodded and asked me questions and I felt like a part of me was healing in the moments talking to her. Like someone understood me enough to not belittle my ideas and trust me with them.

After I stop rambling, she smiles, "I was right."

I look at her and raise an eyebrow, "About what?"

"You remind me of me at your age. Stubborn, hard-headed, and full of hope and dreams. I could dodge any curve ball thrown at me." she smiles. "Have you told Megan yet?" she asks me.

"No, ma'am. I plan on it today." I tell her getting up from the table and washing the orange juice glass I had and putting it up.

"I think she will be on board." She pats my back as she walks past me and towards the den.

"Margaret?" I say and she turns to me. "What is it that you write in that book all the time?"

She smiles, "Something I hope gets read by the person it's intended for someday." She turns and exits the kitchen and starts up the stairs to her bedroom.

I hear a car pull up outside the house and I walk out on the porch, curious as to who it is. A black Audi R8 is sitting in the driveway with dust still floating in the air around it. Stopping in my tracks, my heart sinks.

"Took me long enough to find you." The voice getting out of the car says as he slams the door. Reba sits up and starts growling, the guy takes a nervous step back to his car door.

I pat Reba on the head and whisper, "Good girl." Looking around tensely I don't see Megan, Collin or Logan anywhere.

"What are you doing here, Stephen?" I ask, making my way slowly off the porch. I'm confused on how he found me.

"Did you forget I have a tracking device in that piece of shit car of yours?" he points to my Altima and smiles back at me.

He looks around the place from where he stands and then looks back at me, "What the hell are you doing here, Ivy?" He steps towards me, and I take a step back in response. "This place is not you."

I stare at him, "This is my home now and you are not welcome here. Fuck off, Stephen." I put my arms over my chest, but my eyes don't break his.

"Well, well. Someone has become mouthy from her time away from me. We will need to fix that wont we." He says angrily.

My eyes are pulled back to the car when I hear the passenger door open and see a blonde-haired woman get out. She smiles at me.

"You need to come home!" My sister Courtney says to me sternly.

I roll my eyes at her and cross my arms.

"You have no room to tell me what to do you home-wrecking whore!" I snarl at her.

"Oh, come on, Ivy. Stop being dramatic." Stephen says while taking another step towards me, "What you saw that morning was just a misunderstanding." He gives me a devilish grin. "Don't be a dramatic bitch."

Courtney crosses her arms and stomps, "I seriously question your mind and how it works, nothing happened."

"What I saw was my soon to be husband cheating on me the day of our wedding and my sister betraying me! You never loved me, Stephen. Now go the fuck home!" I yell as I'm turning back to the porch. He grabs my arm and jerks me to his car, pinning me to the front of it. I wince in pain.

"I am not going anywhere without you." He says and I kick at him. His hand goes to my throat, "You will get in this car, Ivy! You do not get a say so." Tears are falling down my face as his hand around my throat tightens. I start seeing stars when, suddenly, he falls to the ground. I look up anxiously and pick myself up off the front of the car slowly. Logan and Collin are both taking turns beating the shit out of Stephen and Megan runs to grab me.

I can hear Courtney screaming for them to stop but she does not move from where she is standing.

"Ivy!" Megan screams and looks at me, "Did he hurt you?" She looks me over.

I shake my head and she pulls me into her. We watch the boys kick, shove, and punch Stephen.

"Jesus!" Stephen says and stands up, blood now starting to run from his nose and a cut in his lip.

"Ivy, stop being a selfish bitch and come home." Courtney screams at me and Megan turns her head towards my sister.

"You better shut the fuck up before my fist messes up that nose of yours." Megan snarls.

Courtney gasps but doesn't say another word.

"Why are you messing with our girl?" Collin says to Stephen, his fist still down at his side ready to throw another punch.

Logan looks at me and Megan, and then to Stephen, "I'm guessing you're the prick who thinks he can cheat on his fiancé on your wedding day with her sister?" He walks closer to Stephen and Stephen cowers.

"The only reason I did it was because the little bitch wouldn't give me what I needed." He pauses, "But her sister sure did. More than just that time, too." he smirks at me.

Courtney laughs, "We had plans to run away together soon after your wedding day. He just wanted the money our mom was giving him to even marry you in the first place." She smiles at me in an almost evil way.

My tears turn into anger, and I pull out of Megan's arms, "You know what, you don't deserve me, Stephen. You never loved me. You were only after my name and my father's money." I pause taking a deep breath while looking at Courtney, "And you, you never were a sister to me! You always thought you were better. Go back where you came from and stay the hell away from here! *Both* of you!" Logan gives me a proud smile and I ignore it, walking back to the house.

I make it to the porch steps before I hear, "Fine. I'll get what I need from your sister. She puts out more anyway. She is less of a bitch, too."

I turn but Logan is already stepping towards him, "She said get the hell out of here." He grabs Stephen by the collar and pulls him to the car with Collin behind him. "So do us a favor, you and your bitch get the hell out of here." He slams him into his driver's door and Stephen falls onto the ground. Courtney quickly gets into the passenger seat and slams the door.

Logan leans down and whispers, "You ever step foot towards her again or come around here and I will personally make sure you are a meal for the coyotes."

Stephen scrambles to his feet and jumps into his car. He drives off in such a hurry, he throws gravel from his tires. Megan walks up the steps with me and we take a seat on the porch swing.

"You okay, Ivy?" Collin says while looking at me like he's checking for wounds.

I nod my head up and down.

"I guess you do care about me." I smirk at him, and he laughs. "You have been a pretty big help around here." He grins and walks off the porch and around the house.

"I'm glad you're okay." Logan says, and he stands for a moment like he wants to say something, but then walks off with Collin.

Megan wraps her arm around me and I lean my head on her shoulder, "I don't mean to pry, but I got to know all the details and this new plan of yours." Megan says as we swing.

I laugh and roll my eyes. Only Megan would not give me a single moment to process what just happened. She *is* making me tough.

"I notice the farm doesn't have its own stud. You would make more if you had your own. What if we decide to use Molly's colt for a stud and start building our own bloodline with him?" I say continuing to tell her about my experience with Rylee and everything with Logan and me.

She looks at me like she wanted to kill Logan and during that whole conversation, I had to physically pull her arm to make her sit back down because she literally said, "I'll kill him."

After a moment she comes to her senses and focuses on the bigger part of the conversation.

"Ivy!" she squeals once I am done with the details, "This is exactly what my uncle and parents wanted to do!" Tears fill her eyes and mine follow immediately after. She hugs me, "I think it's the perfect plan! Our own bloodline!"

She jumps up from the porch swing and takes my hand, "Let's go! You're going to town with me." she smiles.

I laugh, "Yeah right! I have so many chores to get done today. Y'all let me oversleep." I roll my eyes at her.

She puts her hands up in the air as a surrender, "That wasn't me. Logan made us swear we wouldn't wake you up. He has done all your chores and his. Now that I know what happened, I really think he's sorry. Makes sense why he was moping around this morning." She says, grabbing my hand and pulling me to her truck.

"I need to talk to him," I pause, "But.... I'm just not ready yet." I look at her when we get to her truck. "Where the heck are we going?" I ask, still confused.

"I told Grandma I would go into town today and pay on Grandfather's nursing home bills, so she didn't have to get out. She hasn't felt too good while you've been gone." She shrugs and gets in the truck.

I slide in the passenger side and suddenly feel nervous.

"Maybe he's having a good day and I can introduce you." She smiles and puts the truck in reverse as we head out of the driveway.

14

The drive to the nursing home over in Cedarville was only about twenty minutes. The mountains and pastures were just as pretty as they are in Maple. This town seemed to be one that has been long forgotten by everyone also. Everyone except the people who live in it. They are the ones that make it feel like home. Megan and I talked a lot about the farm and our plans for the future. She told me she was worried about her grandmother. She has started having dizzy spells lately and it has worried her and Collin. She slept most of the day yesterday.

The nursing home is smaller than the ones in the city, but big for a town like this. It is the only one within about an hour's drive, according to Megan. She says the staff here are so wonderful and caring.

The sliding automatic doors open at the front as we walk in, and I follow Megan over to the receptionist desk. There is a lady sitting behind it with short, red hair.

"Can I help you?" she asks us with a smile and then recognized Megan standing beside me. "Oh, Megan! Coming to visit your grandfather?" she asks.

"Yes, ma'am." She smiles, "This is Ivy. She's new to the farm and one of my friends. I wanted to introduce her to him if he's feeling well enough, today."

The lady smiles at me and looks back at Megan, "I'm not sure, Sweety. I haven't been down to see him, today. Becky is working his hall. Have someone get her for you at the desk if she isn't there before you go in, just in case."

She gives us visitor passes and presses a button for us to walk inside further. Megan and I both thank her and continue through the now opened entrance to the hall.

The halls are painted in a boring, neutral tone. It is what is hanging on them, however, that make them beautiful. All of the residents have drawn pictures, or created art in some way, and the staff has it all displayed throughout the walls.

We walk past one area, and there are hair stylists rolling and drying some of the residents' hair. I smile at how much they do to ensure they feel that their life is not over being in here. We eventually approach another desk, and a brunette is sitting behind a computer charting. She looks up and smiles, "Megan! I'm so glad you came by today!" She smiles and stands up, coming around the desk to give Megan a hug.

"Hey Becky!" Megan hugs her back, "How is he today?"

Becky gives a soft smile and nods, "He is in one of his better moods, today." She turns to me, "And who is this?" She smiles at me.

"This is my friend Ivy, and a new hire on the farm." Becky shakes my hand and says, "Pleasure to meet you, Ivy. This is an awesome family you are in with." She winks at Megan.

"He's in his room." Becky gestures down the hall to us and returns to her desk, "If you need anything, just come and get me." She smiles and goes back to typing on the computer.

I follow Megan down the hall, and we take a left down another hall. This place is a lot bigger than I thought. I could get lost in here quick.

Megan turns to a door with *321* on the sign, and the name, *Jefferey Landon Mapleson, SR* tagged under it. I smile at the beautiful name. Something I could see naming my son one day.

Megan opens the door slowly and we both step inside with me behind her. If he sees anyone first, it needs to be Megan. The lights are dim inside with television noise in the background. From the sound of guns and hooves, it sounds like he is watching a western. Megan turns on the lights as we walk in, and I notice him sitting in the recliner facing the tv.

He looks exactly like the photo Margaret showed me of the two of them the night I spoke with my mother. He's aged, yes, but not as much as you would think.

The man turns his head and smiles, "Megan, sweetheart. I was wondering when you would be by to see me." He stands and hugs her. She sounds relieved by her exhale. I am sure she thought he would not know who she was.

He releases their hug and looks behind her at me. His eyes widen and his face goes pale like he has seen a ghost, and it almost startles me. Megan begins looking nervous, unsure what he is about to do. She had warned me before we got here how bad his temper has been when he does not remember things.

"Maggie?" he says, walking to me tears filling his eyes and his voice shaky. He hugs me. Megan and I exchange looks of shock. He does not let go. Instead, his hug turns into the biggest, bear hug.

"We never thought we would see you again." He's crying now, and I do not know what else to do other than play into it. I really do not want to upset him.

"Yes, yes. I'm here now." I tell him rubbing his back and he begins sobbing.

"I-I'm going to go get Becky." Megan says, rushing out of the room and part of me wishes she would not have left me alone with him.

He pulls me out of our hug and looks at me, and I feel like he is studying every feature on my face, and my hair. I smile at him to try to hide my nerves, and he cups my cheek, "You look so much like your grandmother." He says and my mouth drops wide open.

Holy shit! Margaret and Jefferey have another grandchild? Why hasn't Megan told me? Wait, what if the child died and Megan never knew about it? It would make sense with his dementia and Alzheimer's.

I think all of this to myself as Megan and Becky come running in.

"Mr. Mapleson," Becky starts as she walks in slowly, "Are you okay?"

He turns to her and smiles, "Never better. My Maggie has made her way back home to me.

I always told Margaret she would." He smiles and pulls me into a hug again.

I look over at Megan and she mouths, "Sorry" to me and I just brush it off. I am simply happy that he is happy. Even if just for a moment. I'm not sure if I should bring the grandchild he mentioned to Megan's attention. What if she did not know about it?

Megan and I did not stay long after we got there. Becky thought it would be best for visitors to come back later because of how emotional Jefferey was.

"I'm so sorry," Megan starts as we get in the truck. "I have no idea who he thought you were." She says while putting her wallet back in her purse from paying Jefferey's bill while we were here.

"I don't know if I need to say this, but I don't feel like keeping it to myself," I say looking at her, "Do you have a cousin or sibling you don't know about?" I ask her.

She looks at me confused, "Not that I'm aware of, why?"

I shrug, "Just something your grandfather said to me." I pause and she looks at me to go on, "He said that I looked like my grandmother." I look at her, "Meaning they have another grandchild. Named Maggie." I say to her, and her eyes widen.

"I wonder if my mom was pregnant with a baby or lost one?" She pulls out onto the main road. "It's only me and Collin, that I know of. My uncle wasn't married or with anyone." She shrugs, "Maybe Grandpa just wasn't as good today as we had hoped."

"Is it just a coincidence that Maple and Mapleson seems oddly similar?" I ask cocking an eyebrow at Megan.

She smirks, "I wonder when you would catch on to that. My family was the first family to settle here."

"Wow." I say to her with my mouth open. "How amazing is that?"

I look out the window and think of the man who was everything I had ever pictured a grandfather would be. My parents were not on speaking terms with their parents, so I never had grandparents who took care of me the way Jefferey and Margaret cared for Megan and Collin.

In another life, I wish I could have had the opportunity.

15

I have been here another week and have not heard from Stephen or my parents. I am starting to think I will never hear from them again. Not hearing from Stephen or Courtney, fine. I do not wish to hear from them. My parents, though? I assumed they cared more than this. Especially Dad.

Molly's colt is growing stronger every day and Megan thinks he will be a big Blue Roan once he finally changes his color. Maggie and her mama are out in the pasture with the other calves and their mamas. It is so cute to watch them take off running and bucking, from time to time.

Logan and I still have not spoken much, other than about chores or the farm in general. I am not even sure what I want to tell him. My heart has been through so much, and parts of me feel like I need to focus on myself, for the first time. I scoop a pile of horse poop and throw it into the wheelbarrow. I swear, I thought over time this smell would get better. Yet, every day I feel like my nose is going to fall off.

The summer heat in Georgia has finally gotten to a miserable temperature and humidity combo, and I feel like this tank top is not enough relief. I need to be in a pool- a *cold* pool.

"Almost done?" Megan asks me, walking into the barn with a saddle hanging on her hips. She puts it down in the tack room and walks over to the stall I am mucking.

"This is the last one!" I say, proud of the hard work as I look around.

"Meet me in my bedroom when you're done," she walks off and then turns back around, "We are going swimming!"

There is not a pool around here, so I wonder where we are going. I also hope she has a bathing suit that will fit me.

I watch her walk out of the barn and I get a sudden burst of energy hearing those words. I fill my last wheelbarrow with manure and dump it in the pile out back, at record speed. I then put the wheelbarrow back in the tack room along with the shovel. Dusting off my hands, Tiny sticks his head out of his stall. I see his hair from his mane floating in the wind. All the horses have fans in their stalls blowing on them when the temperatures rise.

"No ride today, buddy," I rub his forehead, "Stay cool." I kiss him on the nose. Tiny and I have taken evening strolls a lot this past week. Mainly us, but sometimes Megan joins. It has felt freeing, and healed parts of me at the same time. I never knew I could love the life I am living now as much as I do.

Making my way into Megan's room, I stop with wide eyes and notice she is standing in front of a mirror in a bathing suit. "Megan," I start walking over to her, "My ass is bigger than yours. Nothing you have is going to cover me." I say looking nervous.

She waves me off, "Stop your fussing. It will just be us girls anyway." She smiles, throwing me a few suits to try on.

I hurry to the bathroom and shut the door, locking it. I have not made the mistake again of leaving it unlocked, since the Collin incident. Trying on the first hot pink bathing suit, it pretty much fits my ass like a thong. I roll my eyes, the next one looks like it will fit the same.

I grab the black suit and put it on. To my surprise, it fits well. A little snug on the bottom but not as bad as the thong I had on a moment ago. At least this one covers *some* of my ass.

I throw my tank top and a pair of shorts I bought from the store over me, and walk back into her room. I toss her the suits I did not choose

"So, one did fit you!" She smirks, and I roll my eyes.

"Where exactly are we going?" I ask her.

She grabs her sunglasses and a bag with towels in it. "There's a pond on the side pasture. My uncle built a dock on it before we were born." She grabs my hand and leads me out and down the stairs.

"We can drive the truck out there," she says. "Bye, Grandma," she says as she bends and gives her a kiss. "We are going swimming. How are you feeling?" she asks her.

"Didn't sleep well last night," Margaret answers and kisses her back, "But you girls have fun and don't worry about me. I'm going to go visit your grandfather in a little while." She smiles at both of us and continues writing in her book.

Megan and I pile into the farm truck. Megan's bag sits between us, and I notice she brought speakers for her phone to connect to for music. More importantly, she packed snacks.

The dogs stand with wagging tails as we drive away, and I could not feel more at peace than I do now. This place, the house, the farm. It is everything I wish I had growing up. I wish I had never grown up in the city with the strict parents that I did. I wish I had never met Stephen at my dad's law firm, and that I had met someone whose dream was for us to build a life together. I think about Margaret and Jefferey, the life experiences they must have gone through together, and things they have overcome. Losing their children in a terrible accident, raising their grandchildren, working a farm, and not to mention, the time he was in the military and how hard that must have been for Mrs. Margaret while he was gone. I want the kind of love that can walk through the deepest depths of hell and still come out of the flames on the other side holding hands. A love that can overcome anything as long as we are together.

I notice we are in a different pasture than I am used to being in. This pasture does not have a single animal on it. There is large pond in the middle with a dock that goes out close to halfway and another Magnolia tree. A smaller one than the one at the house. Megan pulls up right by the dock and we jump out. I grab her bag and meet her on the end of the dock. "Wow." I say, "This place is gorgeous. Why are there no animals here?" I ask her and she shrugs.

"All Grandma says is this is my uncle's land. He requested in his will that the pond remain, and the land stays clear of animals. We have honored his wishes." She smiles, remembering him.

"Were y'all close?" I ask her. "You and your uncle?"

She wipes a tear from her eye and her lips turn up into a small smile, "I was young, but yeah. He was like a second dad from what I can remember. There's pictures of him somewhere. Grandma put them all up a few years ago, which I'm not sure why. The memory must have been too much."

I smile and nod but stay silent. This family has been through so much it breaks my heart. I wish I could do something for them, but I can hope my presence here is healing more than just me.

I look around at the pond and land, "That would be a beautiful place for a farmhouse." I say, pointing to the far back pasture. The pond would be directly to the right of it and the sun would set directly across the water from the house. That would be a perfect view.

Megan agrees and she walks on to the dock, nearly to the end. I follow her, taking out towels once I get to where she is. I place one on the dock for me to sit on.

I drop the bag and start to sit down, "Oh, no ma'am," Megan says, walking back to the magnolia tree, grabbing a rope I must have missed when I walked past it. "We came to swim!" She walks towards me with the homemade swing with a handle tied to the end of it. She hands it out to me, and I raise an eyebrow.

Standing up, I grab the handle from her hand, and I yank on it a few times to make sure it is secure enough to not break. "How deep is this pond?" I ask her and she smirks, "Deep enough for your skinny ass." She jokes and I stick my tongue out at her. I start running towards the water and let the swing take me out into the air above the pond and let go. Dropping quickly in the cool water, it is refreshing as my head goes completely under. The pond is deep enough that I do not even touch the bottom. I swim back to the surface, laughing.

"Now this is what I needed after mucking stalls. Why are you just now taking me here?" I ask and she laughs, swinging into the pond at the same time with a splash.

When she emerges to the surface, we both float around on our backs and enjoy the cool of the water and the blue sky above us.

"Where was our invite?" We hear Collin's voice from the dock. It startles us so badly that we jump. Logan and Collin walk down the dock towards us. Megan and I look up, and Collin is pulling his shirt over his head and does a cannon ball into the water. I squeal when I realize how close he was to hitting me.

He emerges up from the water and laughs. He starts floating around us and before I know it, he goes under the water and I'm being picked up. As he emerges from the water, I come up with him. Somehow, he is standing flat footed on the bottom and I'm on his shoulders.

"Collin, put me down!" I scream as I hold on to the top of his head.

"Damn, Ivy. Don't pull my hair out!" He laughs and drops me down backwards into the water before I realize what is going on.

I come up from the water and splash him, "Jokes on you, I peed on your shoulders."

Megan and I giggle, and the blood rushed from his face. "You did not!" his face changing to a shade of green now at the realization.

I shrug my shoulders, "Be careful who you mess with!" I wink at him, and he splashes me.

"Come on, Logan!" Megan says, "Join the fun." Megan splashes around and I look up, forgetting that Logan had been standing there this whole time. He looks pissed.

"Nah," he says, turning his back, "I think I'll just go back to the barn and check on everyone." He starts walking away in the direction he came from.

Megan and Collin give me a sad smile and shrug.

"I'm going to check on him." I say to them. I climb up the ladder on the side of the dock and put my shorts back on over my bathing suit bottoms and grab my towel.

Running off the dock to the trucks I scream, "Logan! Wait up!"

He does not turn away but I grab his arm as I reach him. "Are you trying to ignore me?" I say a little bitchier than I had intended.

He huffs and turns to me, "You have been ignoring me all week, Ivy." He turns away from me again, and stomps back towards the barn.

"Don't you dare turn this on me!" I say, matching him step for step even though the tall grass is making my legs itch and I'm in my flip flops instead of boots.

He does not say a single word or answer me as I try to talk to him. Instead, his breathing gets heavier, and his nostrils start to flare. He turns, heading to the back of the barn. I stop in my tracks. I have never been back here before. *Is this where he lives?* I think to myself. I had never given a thought to where he lived, for some reason.

He turns up a flight of stairs and I follow him. "Go away, Ivy." He says sternly, but I do not listen.

He gets to the top, stops at the door, and turns to me, "You are infuriating me!" he says with a dark glare. My breath hitches because I have seen his eyes this way before. I feel like I can see into his soul.

His breathing is rigid, and I look down and notice his hand is on my waist. I realize I am still wet from the water I was just swimming in. He steps closer to me, and I am frozen where I stand.

His eyes go to my lips and then to my neck followed by my breast and then I feel him undressing me.

The sound of a horse kicking a stall in the barn knocks me out of my trance and I step back. His hand falls from my waist. "We need to talk about all of this." I say to him, my voice almost a whisper.

He nods but does not say anything. He just opens the door and gestures for me to step inside.

I shake my head no. "We can't talk here." I say and start walking back down the steps. "We both need to cool down first,"

I grab his hand. He looks at the touch, then back at me with hopeful eyes. "I've been through a lot, Logan. I need to think about my heart." I give him a smile, letting go of his hand. I turn and walk back down the stairs to gain as much distance as I can, before I make a mistake and regret it.

<u>16</u>

I cannot make myself fall asleep. Instead, I lay in my bed and listen to the air unit turn on and off, while the rest of the house sleeps silently. Rolling over, I grab my phone and check the time. It is still too early to get up and start my chores. I let out a sigh and throw the covers off me as I slide out of bed. I grab my house coat that lies on the end of my bed and quietly walk out.

I notice Megan and Collin's doors are shut, as I make my way to the stairs. I pause as I am halfway down, noticing the lights on in the kitchen. I continue down the stairs, more slowly with each step, and turn toward the kitchen. It is then I see Margaret sitting at the kitchen table with a cup of coffee.

"Margaret?" I ask and she looks up at me. Her eyes widen and she jumps out of her chair. Tears fill her eyes, and she runs and hugs me.

"Maggie!!" she cries, "It's you!" My heart sinks. *Oh no, not you too!*

She hugs me tightly, like Jefferey did, and pulls me closer. "Maggie! You came back to us. We always prayed that you would." She pulls back and kisses my cheek. Her sobs and tears start getting louder.

Megan comes running down the stairs, "Grandma!" she says, "What is going on?" She looks at me.

I shrug my shoulders and mouth to Megan, "She thinks I'm Maggie." Megan looks back nervously at her grandmother who is taking out her notebook from a drawer.

She hands it to me, and I look at her confused. She grabs my free hand and squeezes it. "There are more upstairs in my closet- a box full. I wrote them all to you, my sweet, sweet, Magnolia." She smiles at me, and I tear up from her happiness.

"I am going to call an ambulance. Something is clearly wrong" Megan says, grabbing the phone, "She's obviously not in her right mind." Megan dials 9-1-1 and I stand with Margaret while she still holds my hand and smiles at me. I am starting to think Maggie is a real person and someone who they tried to go on living without, for some odd reason.

Collin comes rushing down the stairs in that moment, "What is all the commotion?" he asks half asleep.

"Something's going on with Grandma," Megan says, "I've called an ambulance. Go get Logan." She turns to me as Collin runs out the door, "Can you and him get along long enough to keep the farm alive?" she puts her hand on my shoulder and tears fill her eyes, "We need to go with Grandma." She stands wiping away the tears from her eyes.

I nod teary eyed and give her a sympathetic look with a half-smile. Parts of me wonder if this is what she meant when she mentioned her grandmother has been sick lately. She's been showing signs of Alzheimer's, or dementia, and Megan had not wanted to believe it, until now.

***

Eight minutes is all we have to wait for an ambulance to arrive. They put Margaret on a stretcher and load her in the back while we all watch from the porch. Megan gets in the ambulance with her, and Collin follows behind in the farm truck, leaving Logan and I to tend to the farm. Just the two of us.

Logan and I watch as the truck drives out of sight and he steps off the porch, walking away towards the barn. "Do you want some breakfast?" I ask, breaking our silence. He stops and halfway turns, not looking at me, but nods approvingly at the thoughts of breakfast, even though the sun is not up yet.

I yawn and pull my robe tighter around me walking into the house with Logan not far behind. I pour out the remaining coffee left from the last brew and start a new one. Logan pulls open the fridge door and takes out eggs and orange juice, along with flour and sugar from the cabinets.

I watch him closely and when he grabs a bowl down from the cabinet. I turn to him, "What are you making?" I ask him as I take down a coffee cup from the cabinet above the coffee maker.

"Biscuits." he says softly as though he is afraid to talk around me. He pauses then looks at me, "Do you know how to make homemade biscuits?" I shake my head and pour me a cup of coffee. He gestures at the ingredients, "Come here. I'll show you." I watch as he measures the flour, "Margaret taught me one morning a few years ago."

I watch in amazement as he mixes all the ingredients together. He pours some flour onto the counter and takes the dough out of the bowl placing it directly on the loose flour. He hits it over and over with his fist. He then grabs a cup from the cabinet and uses it like a cookie cutter for a perfect biscuit shape. Once all the dough is shaped, he lays them in a cast iron skillet, greased and ready to go in the oven.

"Wow," I say as he loads all the biscuits in the skillet in a particular fashion. "I have always wanted to ask her to show me, but I never got the nerve. It looks easy." I put my hand on the dough, but at the same time he touches the same place, and our hands meet. Logan's eyes look at me and I stare back. Instantly, the place between my legs starts to warm, and I look away quickly. I can feel his gaze still on me, only breaking away when the preheating alarm sounds. He refocuses on the skillet, and places them into the oven.

I scramble our eggs in a pan on top of the stove. Once they are done, I place them on the table while we wait on the biscuits. We both take a seat at the table, but Logan will not look at me. I sigh and look out the kitchen window, noticing the sun is finally rising.

The house phone and oven timer go off at the same time, breaking the silence and startling us both. Logan gets the biscuits out of the oven while I run into the den and grab the phone. "Hello?" I say quickly, hoping it's Megan or Collin.

"Ivy!" Megan's voice is on the other end, and she sounds like she's been crying. My heart sinks, anticipating the worst.

"Megan! How is she?" I ask and I hear the hesitation in her voice.

"They are doing tests, but she's being hostile. They have had to sedate her." She takes a deep breath and I sigh. "We know for sure they are keeping her overnight, so Collin and I will not be home. Are you okay to take care of everything for us?" I can hear her trying not to cry again.

"Hey, hey, it's going to be okay." I say into the phone, trying to calm her down, "We are partners, remember? Not only that, but you are also my best friend. Do not worry about the farm, I have it under control. You take care of Margaret. Keep me updated." I take a deep breath, hoping I can hold up the end of my deal.

"Thank you, Ivy. I don't know what I would do if I had never met you. You are like the sister I never had." I smile at the thought. She is definitely the sister I wish I had grown up with. *Not* Courtney.

We say our goodbyes and I hang up. Walking back into the kitchen just in time to see Logan putting the biscuits on the table and fixing us both a glass of orange juice.

I smile at the view. If this had been another life, I could see it being a life I would have chosen for myself. Logan and I, together in the kitchen, cooking breakfast before morning chores. Right now, I feel too broken to deserve it.

***

Normally, we distribute our chores differently to even the load between the four of us. However, with Megan and Collin being gone, Logan and I are doubling the work. While I do the feeding, stall cleaning, and take Tiny around the pastures checking fences and the mama and baby cows, Logan is riding colts and fixing things that need to be fixed around the barn. We got an early start once we ate breakfast, and we got a lot of things done. It is another sweltering day. I'm debating on taking my jeans off while I clean these stalls, but then I think about all the places this dust could get, and that makes me keep them on.

I hear a horn honk outside the barn as I am shoveling my last stall. I lay my shovel against the wall and walk out wondering who is out front. It's Logan, and he has a big smile on his face.

"Come on, city girl." He smiles, and I see the Logan that I knew before we went on our trip. "It's hot as hell out here. Jump in. Let's go swimming!"

I laugh as I run to jump into the passenger side of the truck. I am happy to see the guy I first met, and I am not giving away an opportunity to cool off.

"Red Dirt Road" by Brooks and Dunn is playing on the radio, and I let my hand hang out of the window as we head towards the pond with the magnolia tree beside it. The dogs run alongside the truck, following us. I smile looking at Logan, who appears more relaxed now than I've seen him in a while. His tan arm is hanging on the steering wheel and his other arm hangs out the window, feeling the wind as he drives. His ball cap is on backwards and his sleeveless t-shirt really shows off the curves in his muscles.

Peeling my eyes from him, I look at the land in front of us. It is heaven on earth. I have been amazed at this piece of paradise since I arrived. The pond is coming up into view and I, again, imagine what it would look like with a house on the other side. This would be the driveway and I could pasture in this whole place. We could move some of the breeding program to this side. It would be a place I would never want to leave.

Logan pulls the truck up to the dock and he gets out. He pulls a cooler from the bed of the truck. I give him a curious look and say, "What do you have planned?"

He smirks. "We need lunch after all the work we've done." He walks onto the dock all the way to the end. I follow closely behind. "Then we can swim. After waiting twenty minutes, of course." He chuckles at the rule and sits the cooler down beside a bag of towels he has already dropped.

He brought sodas and fixed each of us a turkey sandwich for lunch. I smile at the planning he has put into all this and take a big bite. I am starving. He grabs a bag of chips out of the bag and hands it to me. I smile as I open them and grab a chip, popping it into my mouth.

"May I have a chip?" he asks me with big puppy eyes.

I laugh, "Oh, you have learned your lesson, have you?" I ask, remembering the time we met when he took my nachos without asking.

He grins, "I don't feel like being on your bad side this go around." I hand the bag of chips to him, and he takes one popping it into his mouth. I gulp suddenly, weirdly wishing I was in between his lips instead of that chip.

I think he feels the same way because he quickly looks away toward the pond and gazes over the land. "So…" he starts after a moment, "would you be up to talking to me about Rylee and everything that happened?" he asks but does not look in my direction. He seems nervous, as if this pains him as much as it does me.

I take a sip of my drink and sit it down, taking a deep breath. "I was being a brat." I say first and I think it shocks him because he whips his head to me so fast, I think it could have snapped. "My trauma was still fresh," I sigh, "I was not actually mad at *you*," I take a bite of my chip, "I was mad at myself." This time I avoided looking at him.

He leans on his arm behind him and turns his whole body to me. His eyes glare deep into me. "What do you mean?" he asks, and I tear up.

"I don't know, Logan. I just had my entire world turned upside down and you're a gorgeous guy," I see him put his hand on his chest, playfully acting shocked and attempting to be bashful. I giggle and roll my eyes. "I did not think a guy like you would give me the time of day. I mean, when we first met, you seemed to hate me." I pause to take another sip of my drink. "Then, you let me in telling me about your parents and your emotions. I was truly just trying to find something wrong with you because I'm not used to how you treated me." This time I get an embarrassed blush, "When Rylee kissed you, I got jealous, and I didn't like that you could make me feel that way so quickly." I roll my eyes again when he bats his eyelashes at me. "So, I didn't want to deal with those emotions until I healed my own." I sigh and press my lips together, shooting him an apologetic look.

He stays silent for a minute and turns back to investigate the pond. My stomach does a nervous flip, unsure what he was about to say. Suddenly, he gets up to stand and pulls his shirt off over his shoulders. My heart rate spikes and my eyes scan over the muscles in his stomach. They glisten perfectly in the sun with the sweat running over them. He takes a step back on the dock and runs, landing a cannon ball into the pond, going under the water.

I gasp and stand up fast watching him come back up. "You idiot! You just ate! Get out before you get a cramp! What happened to the twenty minutes?" I scream at him, and he laughs.

"Get in, city girl, or I'm coming after you." He says with a flirtatious smirk. I cross my arms over my chest and shake my head in a determined "no". He swims over to the ladder and right before he grabs it to come up, I put my hands out with a shaky voice, "O-okay." I roll my eyes and lift my tank top off over my head and slide my jeans off, leaving me in my bra and panties. Thank God I wore granny panties.

I follow suit, taking a step back and running, just like Logan, jumping into the pond, going completely under water. The cool water sends a shock to my system. I needed this! When I came back up, I feel a hand go around my waist. I open my eyes and meet Logan's stare as they darken with desire. His jaw is clinched, and his nostrils are flaring. He pulls me to him, and I instinctively wrap my legs around him.

His stare drops to my lips and then back to my eyes. "The only thing I could think of the other day when you were on Collin's shoulders was that I don't want any other guy between these legs but me" he rubs his hands upward along my thighs, and I bite my bottom lip, slowly.

He sighs and lays his forehead to mine, looking down between us. "Rylee and I were serious at one time. We had even discussed marriage but when my mother died things changed. I ended things needing a new start. We were two kids in puppy love, we would have never survived marriage. She was too controlling. I didn't know where she ended up or who she was with. I changed my cell number soon after getting here at the farm because I wanted a fresh start and realized it wasn't going to be with her. Then I met you." He leans his head back looking into my eyes again and continues. "From the moment I met you at

Hilltop, I knew I wanted to be with you." He smiles at me, "Soaked from beer, and all."

We both laugh.

Logan exclaims, "I promise you, Ivy, I haven't been with anyone since we met. I told Rylee how I felt about you when you stormed out of the barn that day. That's why she gave you the refund check. She knew that I was leaving with you. I needed to give her that closure." He says searching my eyes, "I've been yours the entire time."

I didn't give him time to continue, as I plant my lips on his. A deep and passionate kiss that lets a moan escape my lips. I have been praying for this moment for so long and parts of me were unsure it would ever happen.

Logan pulls back from our kiss and trails kisses down my cheeks, my neck and my shoulders. My nipples harden and I think he can sense it by the way my breathing sharpens.

"*Wait!* I can't believe you were jealous of Collin!" I say pulling back from him and splashing him, laughing.

Logan makes a face at my joke and splashes me back playfully.

I think I love Logan Parker.

17

It's been over twenty-four hours since Megan called me with an update from the hospital. They will not be coming home today like originally planned. Collin came by earlier and got a bag of clothes for them and Margaret but did not stay long. He did tell me Megan would not leave Margaret's bedside and she is just thankful she does not have to worry about the farm.

Logan went out to check fences this morning and I came back inside after doing mid-morning chores to clean up in the house and fix some lunch for us. The house has been so quiet since it is just the two of us here. Logan and I stayed in the main house and watched a movie last night. He slept in Collin's room and let me have my own room, understanding it may take some time before I am ready for that next step for us.

I stand at the kitchen sink, slicing tomatoes for sandwiches, when I look out the window really taking in the view. I never noticed it until now, but looking out I can see the pond that we have been swimming in, in the distance. I smile at the daydream I have of how beautiful it would be to put a home there; with kids running around, dogs and horses too.

Ouch. A pain hits my finger and I look down and quickly snap out of my trance. I put the knife down and hold pressure over my finger. I neglected to pay attention to what I was doing and sliced my finger. I grab a paper towel to put over the cut to stop it from bleeding and start opening drawers looking for a Band-Aid.

I finally find one in the last drawer I open. It is next to the pantry cabinet across the kitchen. I grab a bandage out of the box and wrap it around my finger. I start closing the drawer, but I stop. Margaret's notebook she handed me was sitting on top. I had forgotten about it. It must have been in the stuff I cleared off the table when I was cleaning. Taking it out carefully, I walk over to the table and sit down. Opening the pages, I notice they are all handwritten letters.

Starting on the first page, I notice how recently they have been written by the date at the top.

My precious Magnolia,

How I miss you. Somedays I wonder how you look now. You are well into your woman years now and I wish I knew you. Your father had so many plans for you and so many things I hope you are able to experience some day still. Your grandfather asks about you often. I wish I could tell him you made it home to us…but we will continue to pray you do. I don't know why terrible things happen to us sometimes, but I have to believe something better is coming. Life is funny that way, sometimes it throws us curve balls and we have to learn to dodge them. Sometimes we get hit in the process of dodging, but we just limp on towards that next base as fast as we can.

I wish you knew your cousins, Megan and Collin. They would love you so and I daydream about days of you all running this farm together. I know I will never get that dream as a reality, but it gives me comfort.

There are days I wish I had Alzheimer's like your grandfather, then maybe my mind would get me out of the hell of losing your father and your aunt and uncle. I would only remember the younger days and the better days.

I still try to write to you every day…some entries are shorter than others, my hand is failing on me and some days I can't write as much.

I hope wherever you are in this world, you are doing important things that I always said you were capable of. I hope you know how loved you are, and you always have a home here in Maple. I leave the front porch light on every night hoping you find your way back to us.

I love you, Maggie.

-Nana

Holy shit. They do have another grandchild.

Maggie.

I turn the pages, repeatedly. The entries do not stop. It's like she is pouring her heart out into every letter she writes. Some pages even have tear stains on them where she cried while writing.

Bang. The screen door slamming makes me jump out of the book and I look up to see Logan walking over to me. Shirtless, sweaty, and hat turned backwards. *Damnit.* My legs get shaky just looking at him and it makes me forget what I was just doing.

"What are you reading?" Logan asks, coming over and kissing the top of my head before turning to the fridge and grabbing a bottled water from it. I close the book, quickly, and put it back in the drawer.

"Oh," I say, turning to finish cutting tomatoes for our sandwiches, "just going over mine and Megan's ideas for the breeding program."

He nods and looks down. "Ivy! Are you bleeding?" *Crap.* I didn't get the blood up from the counter where I sliced my hand.

I laugh and reply, "I was" I show him my band aid and he looks at me confused. "I was daydreaming about how beautiful it would be for a house to sit out there." I point through the window in the direction of the pond, "and I forgot I was using a sharp object." I laugh at myself embarrassed.

Logan walks behind me, so close I can feel that he is aroused. He moves my hair from the right side of my neck and kisses where it meets my shoulder. My eyes close.

He reaches around me and takes the knife from my hand and lays it down on the counter. He spins me around and then kisses my nose, my cheek, and then my lips. A soft, yet deeply passionate kiss.

When he pulls back, I just smile at him like a love-struck hormonal teenager.

"Heard any updates?" he asks me, walking over to the kitchen table to sit down away from me so I can finish what I was doing while he smirks, knowing the heat he ignites in me.

I grab bread from the refrigerator and bring over the veggies and sliced meat for sandwiches. "Yes," I say taking a seat. "Collin said not much has changed, but they are debating on putting her in the nursing home." I frown. "She's still asking about Maggie." I shrug my shoulder and we eat in silence.

After lunch I go with Logan to the barn to help with the colts and the two new foals born in the past week. It has been a lot of work, just the two of us, and a learning curve for me, but we have managed. It takes hours just to get all the colts ridden, and then cooled down afterwards, in this heat.

"Hey, my big guy," I say walking over to Tiny after I finish checking on everyone else. He sticks his head out of his stall door, greeting me like he has started doing lately. He has become one of my best friends.

"You and me, tomorrow. Pasture check!" I wink at Tiny, and he nudges me, and I take it as an agreement to what I said.

Walking back to the house I notice the lights on in the kitchen and country music is playing inside. Jogging up to the porch, my nose is hit with the smell of something that makes my mouth water. I pet Reba as I walk past her and head inside, taking off my boots just inside the doorway.

Seeing what was going on in the kitchen, I had to blink a few times to assure my eyes were not playing tricks on me. Logan is standing before me with gray sweatpants and an apron on. I swallow at the sight, to keep up with my mouth watering. My legs rub together, instinctively. I walk into the kitchen overlooking the stove trying to see what he is cooking. "Ah!" he snaps his fingers at me and gestures to the table, "You may sit patiently until its done." He smiles and goes back to cooking while I do as I'm told.

He gives me a side eye from the stove and says, "Good girl." I gulp again. "What are you doing?" I ask him.

He walks over to the sink and strains the water from a pot of noodles, running water over them, and then takes them back to the stove.

"I'm cooking dinner for you. For all the hard work you have done the past few days." He brings everything over to the table and sits it all on potholders. It smells amazing and looks delicious. Garlic bread, noodles, and spaghetti sauce with meatballs. My stomach rumbles from hunger – and impatience. He pours me a glass of wine and places a plate in front of me. Then, he grabs my chin, placing a soft kiss on my lips.

As he releases the kiss, he says, "I'm honestly shocked you listened when I snapped at you." He laughs, "I fully expected you to throw something at me." He winks and sits down next to me.

I take a sip of my wine and start to fix my plate, "And what would you have done if I had?" I ask him, but my eyes never leave the food I'm focused on.

He chuckles and says, "Well, I'd spank you." I pause, my eyes shooting to his and I notice the devilish smile on his face. "You wouldn't!" I say jokingly with a gasp.

Logan leans up on his forearms crossed on the table and says, "I would. I told you, I have many personalities." My cheeks blush and my inner thighs heat. I have suddenly lost my interest in the food. My mind wants to feast, elsewhere.

"So," he says, switching my mind out of the picture I had in my head of him spanking me, "I figure we could watch a movie tonight, if you wanted?" He mixes a noodle with the sauce, twirls it on his fork, and takes a bite.

I nod, "What did you have in mind?" I assume he would have some kind of action or scary movie in mind.

He looks embarrassed and I cock a questioning eyebrow at him, "I kinda thought we could go back to my place and watch movies? I bought them all, but I've never seen them. I read the books and really liked them."

I put my fork down and look at him, "You seriously aren't talking about the Harry Potter movies, are you?" I ask with a grin.

He laughs and says embarrassed, "Maybe?".

"How on earth have you not seen those movies?" I say and my mouth opens in shock. "You are a Muggle, aren't you?" I ask and he laughs out loud. It is the best sound in the world.

"I'm guessing you've seen them?" he says knowingly.

"I'd have you know I am a Gryffindor and completely know every line, so you'll be tired of me by the end of the first movie." I say proudly at him and continue eating my meal.

"Oh, this will be fun." He chuckles.

18

Logan's living space is much bigger than I had imagined. It is like a little apartment over the barn. He has an open concept area with a bedroom at the end and a full bath. By the way it is barely decorated, you can tell that this is solely a guy's place. Yet, it is surprisingly clean for someone who has a dirty job like he does.

We are sitting on his couch, and I think I've either scared him or made him like me more by my theatrical reenactments of the movies. We have started the second movie and I am positive he is becoming a huge fan.

I've been lying on his shoulder with his arm wrapped around me and a blanket over us the entire time. Logan's thumb casually rubs my arm and I feel at home for the first time in a long time. This farm, and everyone I have met here, have made these past few months easier than I could have anticipated.

"What's on your mind?" Logan asks me as the movie goes off, but his thumb continues to rub my arm.

I am silent for a moment, not sure how I'm feeling, but then I remember something and look up at him, "Do you remember the day up on that hill when we saved Maggie?" I ask him and he nods, looking at me like he wants to know where I'm going with this.

"How much do you believe what you told me?" I look away from him but quickly look back into his eyes, "You said nothing's random," I search his eyes, "Do you really believe that?"

His eyes twinkle and a soft smile tugs at the sides of his lips. "Honestly, at one point, I didn't." He turns to face me and holds my hand in his. "I used to believe life was a dumpster fire and it's going to shit on you no matter what." He takes a deep breath and then continues, "Then I made my way to this farm and Margaret and Jefferey took me in like I was their own. They taught me things about life that I had only ever seen in movies and books. I found this place randomly, and I knew when I started work here it, in fact, wasn't random. I just couldn't figure out why." He puts my loose hair behind my ear, "Then you came into town. It was like a lightning bolt hit me the night we met. I honestly didn't know what else to do besides be a dick to you." We both laugh at the memory.

"I want what Margaret and Jefferey have one day. That kind of love and marriage." I sigh, "I sure hope she will be okay."

I lean back into his arms, and we sit in silence, both of us thinking the same thing. Hoping Margaret comes home soon.

After a moment, Logan gets up and goes in the kitchen, "Want anything else to drink?" he asks, opening the fridge.

I answer, "No, thank you."

While he's bent over, looking in the fridge, I take it upon myself and make my way over to him. I make sure not to touch him but get close enough to where I'm the first thing he sees when he turns around.

He turns with a bottled water in his hand and his eyes go to mine, then trails down my body. He licks his lips. "What are you up to?" he asks me, and I do not say a word. Instead, I pull my t-shirt off over my head and let it fall onto the floor.

I see his Adam's Apple rise and fall, and he sits his water down on the countertop. He takes a step toward me, and I put my finger up to stop him. "Don't move." I say and I take my shorts off slowly, gliding them down my thighs and onto the floor. My eyes never leaving his.

Seeing me in my bra and barely-there thong, I watch as his eyes darken and his jaw clenches down, making the muscles in them twitch.

"Now, Mr. Parker..." I start walking towards him, "show me a personality I haven't seen yet." His throat bobs again, and he meets me, kissing me softly. He is gentle, but strategic, as if he is calculating the risks of what he is about to do.

"I don't want to scare you off." He says and my eyebrow hitches. "Not possible." I whisper into his ear.

He accepts the unspoken challenge, and in one quick move, he picks me up and my legs settle around his waist. He holds me up with his hands on my bare ass and he is walking us into the bedroom. Logan kisses me before slowly laying me on the bed next to the headboard.

His green eyes darken to brown, in that look I have seen before, but darker. He crawls up me, his legs in between my thighs, and deepens our kiss. I feel him unclasp my bra. My breasts spring free and he throws my bra to the floor. Leaving our kiss, he trails kisses down my neck and shoulder until he gets to my breast.

My nipples are hardened, and he takes one in his mouth and bites down hard. My back arches and a moan escapes my lips. My body remembers him, and I love the way it reacts.

"Where are you going?" I ask him as he suddenly leaves me and the bed all together, making his way to a nightstand that is locked at the top and puts a key in to open the drawer. I gulp when he takes out a blind fold, rope, and cuffs.

Holy hell. He's into the kinky shit. Things I've never done before.

He makes his way over to me and he bends down at my ear, "You told me to show you a personality you haven't seen before, but if I do anything you don't like, say the words and I'll stop." He says kissing my forehead and I nod.

"Say the words, Ivy." He says, searching my eyes like he's afraid I'll run.

"I promise." I smile at him. I give him my hands and he smirks. "What a surprisingly good girl you are." He puts the cuffs on me one by one. He takes his time as he grabs the rope to tie my cuffed hands to the headboard of his bed.

He covers my eyes with the blindfold. It is pitch black and I can't see anything, anymore. Suddenly, I feel like my senses elevate and *holy shit*, I'm wet.

I hear him walk back to the drawer and grab a few more things out of it. He places whatever he got out on the nightstand beside the bed. I feel the bed dip and he's now between my legs again making a trail of kisses up my stomach, my breasts, neck and back to my lips.

I never realized just how much being blindfolded would heighten my senses. Just him kissing me is making me pool with wetness in my panties. I feel him slide back down my body and stop at my panties. He hooks his thumbs inside and slides them down slowly until they are completely off me. Sliding his hand back up my thighs, he trails a finger in between my legs to my opening and I swear to God, I heard him growl. A full-on primal growl that makes me moan with acceptance.

"You are soaked for me," he glides a finger into me and my back arches. He wastes no time sticking another one in. "What a fucking good girl you are." As those two come out, a third finger joins in, and I can feel them stretching me. I moan loudly and my hips start to ride his fingers, needing more of this feeling.

He leans up on the bed grabbing whatever he put on the nightstand, but his fingers remain inside me. A vibrating noise is heard throughout the room and my breath hitches. I've never used toys before. Stephen wouldn't let me, and I was afraid to buy some and him finding them.

"Have you ever played with toys before?" Logan asks me as he rubs my G-spot with his fingers, slowly.

I moan, "N-no." I whisper, struggling to respond through this pleasure.

He drags the toy down my stomach, and brings it lower and lower, stopping just before he reaches my clit. My breathing becomes desperate, wanting – no, *needing* - him to continue lowering it.

"Well, you see," Logan starts, gliding the toy around my thighs. Teasingly close enough to my opening, but not touching the spot I need him to. "Most guys don't like toys because they are insecure. They don't appreciate them." He touches my clit with it and my back arches, but he quickly removes it. My breathing becomes even more desperate. "A real man knows that toys are his friend, and he should work with them to give his woman the pleasure she deserves." And within that moment, he slowly guides it from the top of my clit, downward. I moan at the contact, and he does the motion over and over again. His movements become slower every time.

"A guy who doesn't put his woman's pleasure first," he removes his fingers from me and leans up to kiss me, "Is not a man, but an immature boy who doesn't deserve the pussy he's fucking." And within one swift movement, he puts the vibrator right where I yearned for it, and my body goes insane.

Logan puts two fingers back in me while he focuses the vibrator on my clit, and he hits my G-spot, repeatedly.

I can feel my body tensing and as I clamp down around his fingers, he moves the vibrator in a circular motion around my clit. My back arches, my toes curl, and the moan I release is feral.

Logan removes his fingers and the vibrator quickly and I hear the bed dip, something that sounds like his pants fall to the floor and the bed dips again.

"Ivy," he says with a strain, "I want to feel you bare, do you trust me when I say I'm clean?"

I nod, "Yes. Please." I beg and he growls again.

I widen my legs for him, my breathing hitches again as I anticipate the feeling of him taking me. I remember how big he is from us taking a shower together in the hotel. I know this is going to hurt to begin with.

He lines up his head with my entrance and says, "I'm going to need you to relax for this to work, baby." He slowly guides himself in me and I tense. He's huge and I haven't been with a man in so long. "I'm going to go slow, but I need you to relax, or I'll never fit." He says again and as he slowly gets a little of himself in me, he bends down and kisses me. That helps me relax, and he pushes himself all the way in.

There's burning at first as I feel him stretch me but then the feeling of pleasure takes over. My hips follow his movements. He trails kisses down my neck and then whispers in my ear, "Who knew my good girl was so bad?" That statement starts my arousal all over again.

He starts to thrust harder and harder until we are both panting and moaning together. He kisses my lips and bites the bottom one. I can feel my release coming and he knows it.

He grabs the vibrator he put on the nightstand, turns it on, and places it back over my swollen clit. My body instantly tenses and my orgasm ripples through my body. My eyes roll back and my toes curl. This brings Logan to his breaking point, too. The clamp my pussy has on him from my release, milks him completely.

I had no idea sex could feel so passionate and releasing. Logan pulls the blindfold from my eyes and kisses me softly. He pulls back looking into my eyes, completely sated. "I think

I'm falling in love with you, Ivy." Logan whispers.

I smile, mirroring his look, and feeling, "I think I'm falling in love with you too, Mr. Parker."

19

"Ivy, I'm so sorry I haven't been there in a few days," Megan says on the phone. She called me today to check in and give me an update on Margaret. They still have her in the hospital. She has been hallucinating and calling out for her children. They are quite sure she is going to have to be admitted into the nursing home. Logan and I were going to visit them this morning, but Megan said they will not allow any more visitors since she is not in her right mind. They are also afraid she will get hostile if she's overwhelmed too much.

"Megan, don't worry. We have it under control. You just worry about your grandma." I say into the phone as I pull open a box of journals I found in Margaret's closet while I was putting laundry up.

I want to know more about who this Maggie is. Hopefully I can figure out where she is today and help bring her back for Margaret and Jefferey. Margaret told me the night she thought I was Maggie there were more journals in her closet. Sure enough, I found them as soon as I opened the door.

I hear Megan sigh on the other end of the line. "Well, how is everything? Are you and Logan getting along, okay?" she asks, and I laugh. "Better than okay." I can hear the smile on the other end, "I knew y'all would find your way back to each other." She pauses for a moment, "Once we get Grandma taken care of, I'll be back, and we can start on the breeding program. I think our colt is going to be a star icon, if your plan works." I smile at the thought of the plan succeeding and having Megan by my side.

"Love you, Ivy." She says on the other end, "I'll call as soon as I have another update." As we end the call my heart rate finds an anxious rhythm as I go to open the box. I take the lid off slowly, and I am shocked at the number of notebooks containing Margaret's letters; there must be fifty or more.

I scan through the books, searching for the start of them all. Once I make my way to the very bottom, I find it. I can tell it was put here long ago from the cover tearing at the corners. I note the date, *1999*

Opening to the first page, the first thing I notice are smudges and smears, that I can only assume are from tears, throughout on various words. I can only imagine what Margaret was feeling as she started these letters. Were they simply to release her feelings, or was the intention for them to have Maggie actually read them, one day?

My Dearest Magnolia,

I have found writing my feelings is easier and safer than throwing and breaking things. I am so angry right now. I can't see straight. I understand why your parents chose adoption for you, but I don't agree. Your mother is sick. They are young. They think this is the best chance for you to have the fullest life.

The agreement was adoption on a short-term, temporary basis. We have tried to stay in touch with your adoptive family. Your poor father is beside himself. They won't give us any information on where you are or if you are even safe. We have been threatened if we keep pressing the issue to see you or question your well-being. I hope you know we would go to the ends of the earth for you, if we could. I would sell all we had to find you and bring you home. The farm is sad without you. The horses are sad without you.

I wonder if you're scared and confused or missing us. I wonder if you ask about us or if they keep thoughts of us away from you. Please know how much you are loved and wanted, my sweet Magnolia. I pray I see you again, someday.

Nana loves you and I promise to always keep the restaurant as a reminder of you. You are the inspiration behind the name, after all. The magnolia tree in the yard is also symbolic of you. Your daddy just planted another one by your favorite pond and one day I hope you are able to swing from the tree like he had planned for you both.

I will never stop praying for your safe return, my sweet granddaughter.

All my love,
Nana

I wipe tears streaming down my face as I close the notebook. How awful it must have been to give your child up for adoption, with the intent of it being short-term, then not being able to find her. I wonder how and why it happened. Continuing to scan over the pile of notebooks I laid on the bed, I pick another at random. *2005*. Again, I flip through a few pages but stop at one about a quarter of the way through. I am not sure my heart can take another hit, but I read on -

My sweet magnolia,

It's taken me a few weeks to write, again. So much has happened, and I don't want to tell you about it, but I feel I am doing you a disservice, as your grandmother, keeping this from you even though you may never know.

Your father, aunt and uncle were in a terrible accident, a head-on collision, on their way to a livestock sale. They were excited for their plan to start a breeding program. I was told by the sheriff, after a late-night knock on my door, they were all killed instantly.

I am angry. So angry. My only two children taken because of a stupid person's decision to drive drunk. I am angry that a reckless choice took your dad from you and parents from Megan and Collin, too. None of you will ever have a chance to know your parents.

Oh, Maggie, your father was the son I always dreamed of having. Calm, compassionate, hardworking and he loved his family with every fiber of his being. But most importantly, he loved you with his whole heart. You were his one true love other than your mother.

He had big plans for y'all and this farm. He wanted to build a beautiful home for you to grow up in, by the pond in the back pasture with the magnolia tree. He wanted you to know that nothing in this life comes easy and you have to work hard for your dreams.

He had so many plans for you. I'm so sorry someone else's decision took all of that from you. I still pray you will find your way back to us.

I will write again soon,

Love,

Nana.

Tears stream down my face and I hold the book close to my chest. Oh, what Margaret and Jeffrey have been through, and she still had the love in her heart to open up her home for me. The pure and genuine selflessness of this family touches my soul in every possible way. I want to give back to them the same kindness they have given me.

I pack the notebooks back into the box, and place them back in the closet.

***

I spent the remainder of the afternoon working out a plan for the breeding program to run past Megan as soon as she gets back home and things start to settle down. Papers cover every inch of the kitchen table and if someone walked in they would think I was in a frenzy. I feel like I'm going crazy.

I have not grown up in this life so I am not as familiar with the ins and outs of bloodlines and semen samples for ordering. It can be tricky, but if my mess of papers indicate the amount of research, mixed with all that I have learned through talking with Megan and living here, and the headache I have acquired, this could actually work.

I hear the screen door slam shut and I look up. Logan has a newborn calf in his arms, and he is covered in mud and blood.

I immediately run to him. "What happened?" I ask looking over the calf.

"Get me blankets from the laundry room, I'll turn the fireplace on and lay her in front of it. Mama didn't make it. She was stuck in the canal, and I had to help get her out." He looked emotional and defeated.

I dash to the laundry room and grab blankets and towels. I run back to the den where Logan now sits in the floor with the calf in front of the fire.

"I tried," he said, and his voice broke. "I tried so damn hard to keep them both alive." We rub the towels over the baby to try to warm and stimulate it. Logan looks at me and he looks like he has tears in his eyes. "She calved early. I was out checking pastures and found her laying there. I don't know how long she had been like that. I don't know if this one is going to make it, Ivy."

I grab his shoulder and give him a sympathetic smile, "I'll go get some colostrum from the freezer." We keep frozen colostrum in the freezer for this very reason. It is one of the first things Megan showed me when I started working here. She always said it was an emergency stock in case we lose a mama. If the baby does not get colostrum within a few hours of birth, they don't have as good of a chance to make it because they lose the initial nutrients they need to thrive.

Grabbing a bag from the freezer, I run some warm water in the sink and sit the bag in it to thaw out. I walk back into the laundry room and grab some small calf bottles we keep in the cabinet and sit it on the counter by the sink. I look into the den from the sink, and I see Logan wipe a tear from his eyes. He cares about these animals as much, or even more, than we all do.

Thankfully the hot water does it's job of thawing the bag out quicker than I thought. I empty the bag of colostrum, filling the bottle about two-thirds of the way. Logan hasn't left the calf's side this entire time. He is letting his body heat help warm it, along with the fire.

Putting the nipple on the top of the bottle, I make my way into the den and hand the bottle to Logan. He tilts the bottle and tries to open her mouth. "Please take this" he says to her and we notice her eyes are starting to open. She tries to fight him at first and then to our amazement, she takes the nipple and starts to suck on it.

We both take a deep breath of relief and I take a seat beside Logan and watch the baby calf drink her bottle.

"Let's keep her inside tonight." Logan says and I nod agreeing.

This farm life is certainly not for the weak. I have a whole new understanding and appreciating these last few months. We are surrounded with so much life and death that its almost poetic. Getting to see the creation up close and personal, caring for these animals who depend on us, It is a beautiful thing.

<u>20</u>

I hear whispering as I try to open my eyes and look around. I feel water dripping on my forehead and jump up in a panic.

I hear laughter and my eyes finally focus. Megan and Collin stand over me with a wet paper towel letting it drip on me from above.

"Y'all do know there are perfectly made beds upstairs, right?" Collin asks me with a smirk and Megan giggles.

I look around remembering we fell asleep on the floor with the baby calf last night. I smile when I see Logan curled up in a blanket next to me with the calf. He is snuggling with her and my heart melts into a puddle. I look back at them, "Mama didn't make it and we didn't think little girl would either, but she looks a lot better this morning." I stand up and the calf stirs trying her best to get out from Logan's hold, but his arms keep her down. She makes a little "moo" sound, and it startles Logan awake. We all laugh, and the calf jumps up to walk around.

"Now that's another personality of yours that I love." I wink at him. He gives me a halfway sleepy grin and Collin takes the calf outside.

"What is all of this?" Megan says looking at all my papers on the kitchen counter and I start to have had an internal panic. I did not want her to see these until we know how Margaret is doing.

"Um," I start running a hand in my hair, "It's my plan but I don't want you bothered with it until Margaret is better. I'm going to need help with the bloodlines and semen samples since I don't know them like you do."

I search her face and she smiles. A tear comes into her eye. I walk over to her and ask, "Megan, what's wrong?"

She wipes the tear away and smiles at the paperwork, "Part of the reason Collin and I came home this morning was to get clothes and the other reason was to give you this." She hands me some papers she had folded in her pocket. I look at her, slowly taking them from her and she turns to Logan, "Come in here Logan, this pertains to you, too." I hear Logan approach the kitchen.

She hands me a document.

"Megan…" I tear up and I cannot look at her or I know I will start crying.

"I can't accept this." I shake my head. "This is too much; you have been too good to me. We can wait." I go to hand her the paper back and she shoves my hand away.

"Grandma's diagnosis is confirmed," a tear slides down her face, "She will be going into the nursing home with Grandpa. She has early signs of Alzheimer's." She pauses, and another tear slides down her cheek. She turns to me, and a tear falls down mine. She grabs my hands, "Nothing is random, Ivy." She smiles at Logan who I am sure is where she heard that line from, "and I know, now, why you were sent our way. I need to take care of my grandparents while I'm able. They took me and Collin in as their own. It's the least we can do." We are both bawling our eyes out now and I nod my head, finally understanding and accepting what she is asking of me.

Turning to Logan, I give him the papers. His eyes scan over them and then his eyes turn wide. He looks to me and then to Megan.

"Meg-I-Uh" he begins, and I swear his voice broke, "What does this mean?" he asks, searching both of our faces.

Megan takes a deep breath, "It means I can't be here, but the farm has to go on. I need people here who can run the farm like it deserves to be ran. Life has to go on. There are lives on this farm who depend on us," another tear slides down her cheek, "Grandma had everything signed over to me when she noticed the signs a few weeks ago. I have temporarily put it into your names. I want to sign the breeding program over to you, as *Ivy's partner*. I'm making her the primary on everything, but you know these animals and their bloodlines better than any of us and you care about them." She gestures to the pallet on the living room floor.

"I trust y'all to take this to the next level." She puts her arm around me, and I can feel the tears stream down my face.

Logan's eyes twinkle as tears pool in the corners of them. "Just until you come back, because it's rightfully yours." Logan says sternly.

Megan nods, "We can cross that bridge later. I don't know how long I'll be away. I'm moving into an apartment near the nursing home, so the house is for you both to use. Collin will be coming back and forth as he needs to, but he will be staying with me, for the most part. We will take turns going back and forth checking in and taking care of both of them." Another tear falls down her face.

I give her a big bear hug and Logan grabs a pen and signs the paper. Megan and I sign where our signatures are needed, and Logan hands the paper back to Megan to take it to the lawyer's office.

Megan turns to me, "Grandma is still hooked on this Maggie girl, but I don't remember having a sibling or cousin." She shrugs and I run out of the room. I return with the notebooks I found at the top of Margaret's closet. "I think these will explain it." I give her the box. "I read through a couple, but I think it's only right for you and Collin to read the rest." She smiles as she takes the box from me.

"Y'all don't know how much you both mean to me and our family." She smiles and hugs us both as she walks out the door. We step out on the porch and Collin is walking back from the barn, "I put the calf in a stall. It used the bathroom like normal and took a bottle of regular milk from me. It seems perfectly healthy." He runs up the porch and hugs us. "Thank you both for all you've done. You know you're family." He pulls back and I can see a tear in his eye that makes me tear up. I'm not used to seeing Collin so serious. He is normally the jokester of the group. I rub his shoulder and he turns to walk off the porch, heading to the truck with Megan.

Logan wraps his arm around my shoulder and pulls me close. I cannot imagine the way they are feeling right now. We stand and watch as they drive out of sight.

"Time for chores." Logan says, smacking my ass and running off to the barn. I chase after him.

Under different circumstances, this life with him is something I could get used to.

***

Logan and I finished all the chores for the day and decided we deserved a night out. We agree on Hilltop. We thought it would be nice to go out on an actual date tonight since all seems calm at the farm. Megan asks that we refrain from visiting them at the nursing home for a while. Margaret is not taking the transition well and Jefferey has not had any good days lately.

I stand in front of the mirror in the bathroom putting lipstick on and brushing through my hair. *Hey, I look like a girl tonight,* I thought. A nice change from someone who looks like she plays in horse shit all day long.

Megan told me to look through her closet if I ever needed anything, so I grabbed the crop top I wore my first night to Hilltop and a pair of bootcut jeans. I am really starting to like these jeans the more I wear them. I hear Logan come in the front door and I know he is downstairs. I refrain from letting him wait on me, so I do one last look in the mirror and turn the light off to go downstairs to meet him.

"Wow." Logan says as he sees me at the top of the stairs, "We can totally skip the bar and stay inside tonight." He says, meeting me at the bottom of the stairs. He wraps his hand around the side of my neck and pulls me in for a kiss.

He knows what that does to me and I have to catch my breath. "Stop." I say, playfully slapping him on the chest. "I deserve a night out like a lady!" I smirk at him and wink.

"You haven't acted like a lady since the moment we met. Why change it up tonight?" He laughs and I give him a side eye. He is right, I am far from it. Since the night he met me, I've been able to hold my own. I have even proved his original assumption wrong about being able to handle farm life. If I have learned anything about being in Maple, it's that you have to learn to dodge those curve balls. I smile at the memory of where that came from.

We both get in the truck and "Livin' on Love" by Alan Jackson is playing on the radio as we pull out of the driveway heading towards Hilltop. I smile as I look at him. Jeans, a button up and his brown hair all tussled around on the top of his head. Messy, but *hot messy*. He glances at me out of the side of his eye and catches me staring at him. He puts his hand on my thigh- high on my thigh, I might add.

"Be careful," I say smirking at him, "those thighs may clamp that hand off if you get too high." I smile happy with myself with that statement.

"Oh, Sweetheart, I'm hoping they clamp around my head later tonight." Logan replies as he glides his hand higher on my thigh and digs his fingertips into my jeans. My lady parts instantly heat up and my nipples harden. Damn this instant reaction to him.

Maybe we should skip the bar and stay at home. Fuck being a lady.

***

The bar is so popular tonight that we had to park at Nana's to even get a parking place. Logan jumps out of the truck and comes around to open my door and grabs my hand. We jog across the street and make our way to the front of Hilltop.

We see a few people we know from town, and I smile and wave at them while Logan shakes hands with a few guys he knows.

"Want a drink?" Logan asks me and I nod. "Michelob Ultra?"

He smirks at me, remembering the beer I poured on him. I shake my head with a laugh. While he walks over to the bar, I find a seat at a free table and sit down. I look around and cannot believe how crowded the place is. The smell of cigar smoke is heavier than I remember, and I cough as a guy walks past me puffing on his.

"Just don't pour this one on me, tonight." Logan says with a grin and sits the beer in front of me with a plate of nachos. I smile up at him and pick one up to eat it, "You remembered?" I laugh and I do not hesitate to dive into them.

"I remember that Collin was right." He stares at me as if he is unsure if he needed to say it. My eyebrow cocks in question and he smirks at me again. "You don't play about your food." I giggle and shrug my shoulders.

He slowly goes to grab a bite of nachos and eyes me for approval. I laugh loudly and take a sip of my beer, nodding at him.

"Logan!" a male's voice says, coming up to our table, "What's it been man? Five years?" Logan gets up and hugs the guy. "Good to see you Cane, what are you doing here?" he asks the guy.

"Night out with the girlfriend. We were just passing through. Big sale going on down the road." He points to a girl who is standing at the bar talking to the bartender and I roll my eyes.

Rylee.

"And who is this?" the guy asks, looking at me like he is undressing me. He makes me extremely uncomfortable.

Logan slides an arm around me, sensing my unease and says, "This is my girlfriend, Ivy." I look up at him because it's a shock to hear those words. I mean I knew we were a thing but hearing those words makes it official. I smile up at him. The guy is looking at him in shock and says, "Wow, man. She's beautiful." He winks at me.

"Hey baby!" Rylee says, coming into view and her eyes widen when she sees me.

"Babe," Cane starts as he turns to me and Logan, "Do you remember Logan? And this is his girlfriend, Ivy." He points at me.

She puts on her best fake smile and says, "Oh, hey! It's so nice to meet you, Ivy." For a moment I don't say a word, and Logan doesn't take his eyes off of me.

"Oh, cut the shit." I decide to say to her, and Cane looks at me surprised. "She knows who I am. We met about a month ago at the farm she works at. She missed out on a hefty chunk of change due to cussing me as soon as I got there." I smirk at them. "Isn't that right?" I smile at her.

"I'm terribly sorry for that." She says and I can tell it hurts her to say those words, "It was a misunderstanding, and it won't ever happen again." she gives me a genuine smile. "I would love to work with you in the future." She reaches out her hand for me to shake.

I stare at it and back at Logan, "We will let you know but for now, we will pass. Excuse me, but I need to talk to Ivy." He says, pulling us away from the main floor area down a dark hall.

"Logan, Wh-" And before I can finish my sentence, his lips are on me pulling my leg up around his waist. He unbuttons my pants and slides his hand down my panties and my breath hitches.

"What a good girl you are being so wet for me." He kisses me hard, and I moan into his mouth. He holds me under my ass as I wrap my legs around his waist, holding myself around his neck. Opening the door to a bathroom with his spare hand, he walks us inside and closes the door behind us, locking it.

Sitting me on the sink, he pulls his shirt off and his dark eyes hold mine, "I want you right now, Ivy." I nod in agreement and pull my pants and panties off. He watches me with fire in his eyes as he undoes his jeans and pushes them down just far enough for his dick to spring out. The veins that run the long shaft are thumping hard with desire and it makes me more wet just looking at it.

Grabbing my hips and pulling me to the edge of the sink, he takes me in one big thrust. I scream out his name and he kisses me. I bite his bottom lip and he growls. He is thrusting in and out of me hard and fast. I lean my head back as my eyes roll back in my head on the edge of my orgasm but needing more to push me over the edge. As if Logan is reading my mind, he takes his thumb and presses it over my clit, circling. That is all I needed to release and my toes curl as I moan his name as loud as I can. The reaction my pussy has, clamping tightly around his dick, causes him to release inside me. Finishing, we both stand there, kissing and breathing sighs of satisfaction, before he pulls out.

"Not that I am complaining, but what was that about?" I say, staring into his eyes, still breathless. "It turns me on seeing you stand up for yourself." He says, brushing the hair out of my face and kissing my forehead. I smile. "And here I was thinking I was just bitchy for pouring my beer on you the night we met. Who knew it would've twisted something primal in you?" I pull my jeans back up and Logan puts his shirt back on and buttons his jeans.

He walks over to me and grabs my chin and rubs his thumb on my cheek, "Even that night, I wanted to bend you over the table and fuck you." I gasp and he laughs, kissing me again softly.

21

Tiny watches me closely as I muck the stall beside him. He is the goofiest horse I have ever met, and he is glued to me every chance he gets.

Cleaning stalls is seriously the part of chores I hate the most and the one I procrastinate for the last part of the day whenever possible.

It has been a few days since we went to Hilltop, had sex in the bathroom, and left to come home to do it all over again in our bed. I catch myself reliving the moment in my head as I scoop up each pile.

I hear a car pull up at the house and it does not sound like Logan's truck. The dogs are barking like crazy, so I know it is not a familiar vehicle to them. I put down the shovel and rub Tiny's head as I walk past him towards the end of the barn. The sun is bright and blinds me as I step out of the barn towards the house. Blinking a few times, I finally notice the car that pulled up and I stop dead in my tracks.

"Dad?"

My father is stepping out of his car and looking around. I walk towards him, confused and looking around seeing Logan's truck but not seeing Logan anywhere.

"Dad?" I say louder, getting his attention. He is dressed like he just left work. A suit and tie with dress shoes.

"Ivy!" he says, shocked at my appearance, "What on earth have you been doing?" he asks me, looking at the dust and mud on my jeans.

"Muc -- cleaning stalls," I say, "What are you doing here?" I ask, confused.

He clears his throat and says, "Stephen told me where I could find you." Of course he did. He looks around, "This is a beautiful place."

He's trying to change the subject on me, and it confuses me even more. "Where's mom?" I ask him sternly.

He looks nervous, "I came alone. You know how your mother is, Ivy. She's still not happy about the wedding and how you ran off." He states, shuffling his feet with his hands in his pocket.

"And you?" I step forward, "What did you think about it?"

He clears his throat again and that is when he pulls his hand out of his pocket. I notice it's bandaged. Seeing where my eyes went, he rubs his knuckles with his other hand, "I made sure Stephen would not be a problem for you again. He has run off with Courtney and we haven't seen them since." He lets out a breath like he's been holding it, "I am so sorry that I did not come sooner, sweetie. Your mother lied to me about your phone. She said you turned it off so we couldn't find you. If I would have known she did it, I would have been here sooner."

In that moment I run to my dad and bear hug him, tears falling down my face. "I've missed you, Daddy."

He hugs me back, but I feel hesitation in his embrace. I know there is something else going on. Looking up at him, I ask, "What's wrong?"

He runs his hand through his hair and shifts nervously. I am now nervous myself. "Can we sit down and talk, sweetheart?" he asks, gesturing to the porch. I nod and walk with him towards the swing.

"You look happy." He says as we sit down, and he brushes my hair out of my eyes. I smile but my eyes tell him to finish saying what he came here to say.

"I love you, Ivy. I need you to know that because after what I'm about to tell you… you may not feel the same about me." He looks down as if he is ashamed of something and my gut gets a knot inside it.

Logan comes walking around the side of the house and my dad looks and sits up straight, "Who are you?" He speaks, protectively.

Logan walks up on the porch, but taken aback by his words, mirrors my father's tone. "Id like to ask you the same thing. That's my girl you're sitting near. Care to state your intentions?" He steps towards me, and I grab his hand.

"Logan, this is my father." The tension eases in both of their faces as they calm down. Logan brushes his hand off on his pants and reaches out to shake my father's, "Nice to meet you-" he looks at me, "James," I tell him, "James. I'm Logan Parker"

Logan nods and my father shakes his hand. I notice the attempt to twist their hands in dominance, but Logan stands his ground. They release when my father chuckles, surrendering. "You got my approval boy." He sits back relaxing in his seat.

"Do you need anything Logan?" I ask him, "My father was needing to speak with me about something." Logan, understanding the need to be alone with my father, shakes his head and bends down to kiss me on the lips deeply. "Sir." He says leaving and nods to my father.

"Quite the guy you've found, there." My father says as he watches Logan walk to the barn.

I smile, "He's everything I could have ever dreamed of. He sort of reminds me of you." My dad looks uncomfortable again and he turns to me. "I need you to understand what I am about to give you is not because I do not love you. It is because I do. Ivy, I want you to know, you will always be my little girl." He looks at me for a moment and then kisses my forehead.

Reaching into his jacket pocket he pulls out a large envelope. It looks old and worn. Tears prick his eyes, and he hands it to me. "I do not want you reading it until I leave. All of the information you need is inside. Please remember, darling, I love you and nothing in this envelope changes that." He grabs my hands and stands before walking towards the end of the porch. "You belong here, Ivy. More than you know. I am amazed this is where you ended up." He pauses, "I'm so proud of you. Call me when you get done reading it if you can. I love you." He turns and walks off the porch, opens his car door and he's gone faster than he came.

I'm confused, looking down at the bulky envelope in my hand. It's addressed to my parents. There is a set of keys I can feel from the outside, a few documents and something else that feels like a thicker piece of paper.

I take a deep breath and open the envelope. Turning sideways in the swing, I dump everything out and take it all in. There is an envelope that says, *Open me first* on the outside. I grab it and open it to find a handwritten note on a few of the sheets. It's written in pen. I unfold it even though I am still confused and start reading the first line.

My dearest Ivy,

I am so proud of you. The woman you have turned into and the self-respect you have for yourself. You are a daughter that would make any father proud, and I hope you know how much you mean to me. From a little girl that sat on my knee while I read her bedtime stories to this fierce woman making a way for herself in this world. I always knew you were capable of many wonderful things.

I knew this day would come and I have been dreading it. You see, there are some things you do not know about and that is mine and your mother's fault. We were selfish in our love for you. We wanted you all to ourselves. Your mother and I tried for years to have children with no success. We were desperate for a family of our own. Your mother went through so many treatments and I even got tested a few times, but luck was not on our side.

One day, after we decided adoption was the only option, we put our name in a database for adoptable children. That is how we found you. A few years after we adopted you, we adopted Courtney from a single mom who was not ready for *children. In my eyes, biology does not matter. You two are my daughters.*

I am so sorry we kept this from you. We had plans to tell you when your biological father got his finances situated. He and your mother were not married. I know little about them, but we were told they were high school sweethearts. They put you up for adoption because your mother was terribly sick and could not care for you. Your father was in the process of starting things for the future. They wanted you to have a stable life and home, away from the ways of their farm, and sickness. Your birth mother died shortly after we adopted you, but your father and I made an agreement that we would return you to your home with him as soon as he got his life stable enough for a child. It was supposed to be an adoption/fostering agreement. Unfortunately, a terrible accident happened a few years after your adoption with us and your father passed away. Like I said, we were selfish and never reunited you to your home with your grandparents. We legally changed your name and removed any photos and pictures for you to remember them. Your father sent me things he wanted you to have before that happened. These are not my finest moments and I regret it all. I guess in a way, I let your mother call all the shots.

Ivy, your given name from your biological parents is Magnolia Rose Mapleson, and you are the granddaughter of Margaret and Jefferey Mapleson.

This is the hardest thing I have ever done but I knew when Stephen told me where you were, I had no choice and could not keep this from you any longer. Your mother does not know that I have made this drive, and I will tell her when I get back home. Right now, this is something, as a father, I should have done a long time ago. Your mother has always wanted to keep this from you, but I do not believe it is the right thing, anymore.

I am sure you have a lot of questions and most of them are in this envelope. Along with some handwritten notes from your biological parents. A copy of his will is included and keys to his safety deposit box. He sent me copies of everything when you were adopted in case anything happened to him. I have had them all hidden in my safe in case this day came.

I want you to know we only thought we were doing the right thing keeping you to ourselves, but now, I am seeing how selfish we were. I will understand if you are angry with me, but I ask for your forgiveness and maybe one day I can still walk you down the aisle and give you away on your wedding day.

You are a strong woman and I admire you for that. I find it no accident that you ended up here, where you were always meant to be. You didn't know where you were heading but a part of me feels like your dad in heaven was the one guiding your car. Take your time to process all of this.

I love you sweetheart,

Please call me.

-Dad

I wipe tears from my eyes as I look up from the letter.

I'm Maggie.

I look out across the porch where the dogs lay before me, sleeping and resting. I scan my eyes over the land and look to the barn. Tears start flowing more as the emotions take over me.

Home.

This is *my* home.

My heart feels like it could burst out of my chest, and I pick up the thick paper that I felt in the envelope and realize it is my original birth certificate. I see footprints on the bottom of the paper.

I scan over it and try to control my breathing.

Name: Magnolia Rose Mapleson

DOB: April 28th, 1995.

Weight: 6lbs

Length: 12inches

Scanning through the rest of the documents, I see the papers from my adoption and all of my parents' signatures.

I notice there is another handwritten letter. *Magnolia,* is written in the crease of the paper in pen. I open it up and see its dated in 1999.

Magnolia,

As I sit here watching you sleep, I wish things were different. I wish I was going to be here to see you experience life. I wish I was going to be here to see you ride all the horses by yourself and give your daddy a run for his money. I wish so bad I could be here to give you boy advice and yell at you for being a brat in your teen years. But as luck would have it, I won't be here physically. I was diagnosed with a rare form of blood cancer and the doctors say it's untreatable. I will be leaving my earthly body soon and will get to see heaven.

Your daddy and I have decided to put you up for adoption. It was one of the hardest decisions I have ever had to make. You are my greatest blessing alongside your daddy. You both make my world go around and if I knew I could beat this, I would try like hell. But Maggie, I am sick, and I don't want to put you guys through anymore heartache.

The sweet couple who has agreed to adopt you have agreed to bring you back home once your daddy gets the breading program off the ground. It is his dream. I hope they stay true to their word for your daddy's sake. He would burn the world down for you, Maggie, if you needed him to. He loves you so much. We both do.

You are strong. You are beautiful. And you will do wonderful things in this life. I will be watching your every step. And every time you are sassy or a brat and then stub your toe or hit your head, know it's your mom hitting the manners back in you from heaven.

Your grandmother has this saying that has always stuck with me: When a curve ball gets thrown our way, we have to dodge them and even if we get hit, we keep going to that next base as fast as we can.

Maggie, even if you are crawling towards that next base, keep going. One step at a time. You will get there.

There is so much I want to say to you and things I want to give life advice on, but I can't. What I can tell you is that one day when you make it back to Magnolia farm, let it teach you lessons you have never experienced before. Let the animals give you much happiness. Let the seasons changing give you perspective on when to go fast and when to slow down.

I dream of the future, picturing what it would be like seeing you on the mountains of the farm, beside your daddy on the back of your horses and smiling big looking at your castle down below. At least, I hope you love horses or your daddy might take that hard.

Please don't do anything halfhearted and don't let down your self-respect for anyone, especially a man. If he loves you, he will show it. No questions asked.

Your daddy loves me fiercely. He is never shy about it and is always showing me how much he loved me from day one. He is patient and kind but also protective and will confront anyone when it comes to me and you. I pray you find that love one day and don't settle for anything less. Someone who will be the best husband and best friend to you but also the best daddy for your children.

There will be sad days, but thankfully there will be happy days, too. Embrace them both and don't forget to laugh often. Life's short. Don't sweat the small stuff.

I will always be with you, Maggie.
Love,

Mom.

Tears are dripping off my chin like a waterfall as I pull myself out of the letter. Wiping my eyes, I see Logan walking out of the barn and he notices I'm crying. He runs to me and when he gets to the porch, he looks at me full of concern wiping my tears away.

"Ivy," he says, scanning my face and looking down at the papers I have displayed all over the swing. "What's wrong? What's going on?"

I hope he's ready for this curve ball.

22

"Holy. Shit." Logan says as he reads over the papers and letters. We came inside from the porch and are sitting at the kitchen table. My mind is on auto-pilot. I think I may actually be in shock.

I am adopted. This whole time and I never had a clue.

"Well, I'll tell you one thing," Logan leans on his forearms towards me smiling, "You look more like a Maggie than an Ivy to me anyways."

I laugh and roll my eyes at the same time. "This is serious. My whole life has been a secret." I feel the tears starting again and I wipe one away as it falls down my cheek. Logan grabs my hand, "This makes so much sense. I told you, nothing is random." He gets up and pulls me up to him in a big hug. I lose it and let the tears fall. I am sure if I were to look in the mirror, my eyes would be swollen red from all the tears.

"I'll get you something to replenish those tears." Logan says to me as I sit back down, looking over the papers.

I hear him go to the fridge and pour a glass of tea in a cup and place it back down in front of me. Only then do I see another handwritten letter in a zip lock bag with keys.

Pulling it out, I look at the date at the top… *2005*.

Magnolia,

I feel like it's almost time for you to come back to us. Your uncle, aunt and I are leaving this weekend for a sale to bring home some big-time bloodlines back to the farm. Things are about to change for us, baby girl, and we will be a family again someday.

I dream of the day I teach you how to run this farm and you and your cousins play in the yard, swim in the pond and get into mischief.

My plan is to get you a big chestnut gelding one day for you to check pastures with and who will protect you when I'm not around. I can picture it now. You two will be best buds and give any farm hand a run for their money.

I miss you so much, Magnolia. You are the light of my life and I dream of the day you are in my arms again. This past year, I planted a magnolia tree by our pond with you in mind, and my hope is one day you are able to swing from it in the summertime.

Magnolia Farm was named after you by your grandparents. The part of the land that belongs to *me will be yours someday. It's all included in my will. My will is included in these papers.*

The life I live is dangerous, so if for some reason we don't reunite, I need you to know some things… The keys in the bag with this note are for the safety deposit box at the bank in Maple. All my money is to be yours when you turn eighteen. If something happens to me and your aunt and uncle, when your grandparents pass, the farm will be split three ways between you and your cousins. You each get your own plot of land plus the main farmhouse is all of yours to do with what you wish.

Nana specifically has the diner in your name to be yours when you come of age. I'm sure she has changed some things by now in case you don't return to us, but I sure hope you do. I pray every night I will see you again.

You would love it here, Maggie. I've built it all for you. Other than your mother, you are my main love. My heart burst open the day you were laid in my arms for the first time and looked up at me with those ocean blue eyes. Same eyes your mother had. God, I miss her. I want you to know I loved her so much. She was my best friend and the person I wanted to share this life with. What I would give for us all to be a family again. We wanted you to have the best life and that is why we made the decision for another family to have you for the time being. It is not a permanent situation. At least I pray it's not. The breeding program is going to take off, I just know it.

I hope you meet your grandparents one day. They are the strongest people I've ever known, and I hope you get that fight in you. To keep going even when life gets tough.

I will always be waiting for the day that you are back in my arms again.

Love,
Daddy.

I am unsure how I got here but I am in Logan's arms and he is rocking me. The tears just will not stop. I'm sad, angry and shocked. I mourn the life I could have had. The life that I have wanted the whole time I have been here on the farm.

My farm.

Tears stream down my face as I think about Margaret and think about how even before I knew she was my grandmother, she treated me like one of hers. I may not have had her growing up, but these past few months gave me a little bit of that life I dreamed of having with a grandparent.

And Jefferey, when he hugged me. He was the first to call me Maggie.

He knew.

Tears come down faster and Logan says "shhh" to calm my breathing. I think he is in as much shock as I am.

BANG.

I hear the screen door fly open and Megan comes running in. She has been crying and my heart sinks. Don't let this be bad news. I haven't even got to tell them yet. She stops as soon as she sees me and wipes a tear from her cheek.

"You're Maggie!" Megan says running to me and squeezes me.

We both stand there sobbing. Logan stands by us but lets us have our moment. Collin comes running in after a moment and he wraps his arms around Megan and me.

"I told you that you were family." He says to me, and I laugh and cry at the same time.

I look at Megan and then back at Collin confused, "How did you know?" I ask. They look at each other and smile.

"The letters Grandma wrote. They told us everything. You must have not read many of them or you would have figured it out, too." She grabs my hand and squeezes it, "There was a copy of your birth certificate and adoption papers in one of the books and it had all their signatures with it. I put it all together by the last names." She smiles at me big.

Logan comes up behind me and wraps his arms around my waist, holding me close to him.

"Have you told them?" I ask Megan, and she shakes her head.

"That's why we came to get you. We want you to be the one to tell them." She squeezes my hand again, "They are both having a good day, let's go." I nod looking at Logan and he nods with me and releases my waist. I grab all the papers from the kitchen table and bring them with us to the truck.

***

Logan and I follow Megan and Collin in his truck to the nursing home. The tears have finally stopped, but my stomach feels like I could vomit. I am so nervous. What if I'm not the granddaughter they wish I would have been. What if they are not in a good headspace when we get there? I wish I could rewind so much but still know what I know now.

Pulling up to the nursing home, Logan parks beside Megan in one of the first parking spots close to the door. The four of us get out of our vehicles and walk together through the door. Megan drapes her arm around me.

Checking in at the receptionist's desk, the woman looks at us and smiles. "Need names for the visitor badges for you two." She points at me and Logan.

I smile, "Maggie Mapleson." I reply to her finally saying my full name out loud and the woman looks up at me, shock in her eyes, and then they glisten with tears.

She turns to Megan, and she nods in confirmation, then smiles. Before I am aware of what is going on, the receptionist is running around her desk and grabbing me in a hug. She cries, "You came back home. Your grandparents have been praying for this day." She rocks me back and forth in our hug.

"Were you not here a little while ago with a different name?" she asks, pulling away from me and looking at Megan. "Long story." Megan says, "But this is Maggie. We actually just figured it out today, so we are here to tell Grandma and Grandpa." She smiles at me.

The woman is gleaming with excitement and tells everyone in the room about me. They all walk up and hug me as if they have been waiting on this day, too. Most of them are wiping tears.

She prints off our name tags and hands them to us. We peel off our assigned stickers and place them on our shirts. She hits a button for the main door to open into the hallway and we all walk in, following Megan down the hall.

Megan stops at the nurse's desk and asks for Becky- the nurse I was introduced to the first time I was here.

After a moment, Becky walks into sight from one side of the hall.

Megan runs up to her with a smile, "Becky I need to introduce you to someone." She smiles at me, and Becky looks at me and then back at Megan, confused. "I met her a few weeks ago. Ivy, isn't it?" she asks me.

Megan replies, "Well, yes, but also, no." Becky looks confused. "This is my cousin, Maggie. We just found out she is adopted, and they changed her name."

"And kept her from us like kidnappers." Collin chimes in and Megan rolls her eyes at him. I giggle, thankful to see him joking again.

Without a second thought, Becky grabs me and hugs me. A full-on bear hug, and when she pulls back, tears glisten in her eyes.

"You look so much like your mom." She touches my hair and I smile. "You have her eyes. How did I not notice it before?" a tear falls down her cheek.

"You knew my mom?" I ask her with tears in my eyes.

Becky grabs my hand and squeezes it, "Your mom was my best friend in high school. I was the first person she told when she found out she was pregnant." She smiles, "Well, other than your dad, of course."

She hugs me again, "Margaret and Jefferey will be so happy to see you." she wipes a tear, "You find me if any of you need anything."

I nod and give her one more hug.

We make our way down towards their room. They added Margaret's bed into Jeffrey's room to keep them comfortable and familiar when having any episodes.

Opening the door, Megan and Collin walk in first and Logan and I follow closely behind.

The room is lit by lamps and the light from the television. Margaret sits on a recliner farthest from the door and Jefferey sits in the other. Turning to face us, Margaret's face lights up and she says, "We have visitors, Jeff." He turns to her and then back to us as if it takes him a minute to understand her words.

"Hey kids!" he says, turning down the television so he can hear us.

Megan walks up to him first and kisses him on the forehead.

"Grandma, Grandpa, I found someone who wants to come visit." She turns to where I come into view and both their faces light up.

Margaret cannot get out of her chair fast enough to pull me into a hug.

"My sweet, Maggie." She hugs me tightly, and tears roll down my face. Jefferey's arms go around both of us and I am sobbing by the time his arms wrap completely around us.

"Our girl came home, Margaret." He says crying.

I look over at Megan, who is wiping tears from her face. I notice Logan and Collin standing wiping their own tears.

"How did you find us?" Jefferey asks as he pulls back out of the hug.

I look at them, unsure of what to say, unsure if they will remember. And then I look at Margaret and smile, "I just kept dodging curve balls. Every time one would hit me, I kept going towards that next base."

Margaret's eyes sparkle and she smiles big, "You've read my letters."

Happiness is all that fills the room.

23

It's been two weeks since I found out who I *really* am. After we left the nursing home, Logan took me to the bank. I opened my father's safety deposit box he left me. I now have more money than I know what to do with and acres of land in my name. I still haven't decided if I want to contact my parents or if I ever will.

I have woken up every morning thinking I was dreaming just to be thankful I did not need to wake up from it. It's real. Every bit of it. I have cried so many happy tears, and sad ones, too. I think the grief of what could have been has taken a toll on me more than anything.

So many things I always felt were missing. I wish so badly I could have had the childhood that Megan and Collin did, but I live for the stories they tell me.

I have not been back to the nursing home much, other than just a few times. I feel like my place is this farm. Megan and Collin grew up with our grandparents, they need all the time they can get with them. Both have declined a lot lately. Their minds have reverted to their earlier days and they do not remember much of the farm or recognize us. I am having to come to terms with not having the option of knowing them as the grandparents I could have had.

I am sitting at the kitchen table in the house looking over bloodlines for the breeding program. We pick up our first round of semen Logan ordered this weekend, and I am anxious for the outcome. I have decided my place is on this farm, taking on my father's legacy and making his dreams come true. Not just for him but my aunt, uncle and cousins too. It is becoming a dream of mine as much as it is theirs and Logan has become an immensely helpful partner to say the least.

He knows so much about these animals. I become more impressed with every piece of advice he offers. I look to him when it comes to who needs to foal this year and which bloodline to choose. I am slowly getting a grasp on things, with his guidance and input.

I get up from the table and grab a water from the fridge. When I close the door I jump, "Logan!" I say with my hand on my chest. "I didn't even hear you come in." He had been out in the barn the last time I checked.

He moved to me, and I notice the smirk on his face. His eyes are looking at my lips and then back to my eyes. I back up from him as he stalks me until my back is pushed up against the counter.

His arm slowly wraps around me, and he takes my water from my hand and sits it behind me. He puts his hands under my cheeks, cupping them, and he pulls me into a kiss. I kiss him back deeply and he pulls away slowly.

"I think you are too stressed." he says, grabbing my waist and lifting me up on the counter. I gulp. "And I need to shower. So, let me show you what your body needs to relax." I gasp in return and nod at that same time. He smiles and steps in between my legs. I wrap them around his waist, and he gently picks me up and holds me up by bringing his hands around my ass.

"Good girl." He says and walks us out of the kitchen and up the stairs. The ease in which he is carrying me makes me assume I must feel like a feather in his arms. He takes the stairs two at a time and kicks the partially open bathroom door all the way open with his foot. He sits me down on the counter of the bathroom sink and kisses me again. Pulling back, he takes his shirt off over his head and lets it fall on the floor. He walks over to the shower and turns it on, then walks back over to me. Lifting my shirt off, he lets it fall to the floor with his. He reaches behind me and unclasps my bra. My breasts free from it in an instant and he bends down, taking the hard nipple of my right breast into his mouth and sucking on it. I lean my head back in a moan as he moves across my chest to the other one.

He helps me off the counter and I unbutton my jeans and let them slide down my legs, along with my panties. He takes his jeans off and boxers, too. All our clothes pile up on the floor by the bathroom counter.

Grabbing my hand, he leads us both into the shower and lets the water fall over me. His grin turns devilish as he moves closer to me. Picking up one of my legs he drapes it around his waist and with the opposite hand he trails it down my stomach and right before my opening between my thighs.

My breathing grows heavier with anticipation, and he grins at me knowing how turned on I am. Trailing his fingers over my opening he kisses me while pushing one finger inside. My lips part and I moan into his mouth.

"Always so wet for me." he says into our kiss and suddenly I feel another finger slide inside me. This man knows what he is doing, and he is damn good at it.

Tilting his fingers up just slightly, I feel him hit my g-spot and I moan loudly. His cock get harder as it touches my stomach and I smile at the thought that his body responds to mine as much as mine does to his.

It is one hell of a turn on.

He turns the water off and picks me up, "Fuck this." He says in a growl and carries me out of the shower and out of the bathroom.

"What are you doing?" I say hoarsely but laughing at the sudden change of scenery.

He walks us out into the hallway and then pushes my bedroom door open with his leg. He walks us over to my bed and lies me down while he crawls up me trailing kisses.

"I want to make love to you, Maggie." He says to me, and tears glisten over my eyes.

No one has ever told me that before.

He searches my eyes, "Is that okay? To make love to the woman I love?" he says with a grin.

I grin back and grab his head pulling him to me to kiss him. "I love you, too." I tell him and the sound that came from his throat was almost primal. Like an instinct wanting to take over. I spread my legs, and he drives in me in one movement. I feel myself stretch for him as though my body was ready for him. He kisses me passionately as he moves in and out of me, hard and fast, yet, slow and calm. My back arches as he hits the perfect spot and I feel my body tense.

"Not yet" he says, and he pulls out of me and turns me around. I'm on my knees with my ass in the air and head down in the pillows. In one big thrust he is back inside me, and I moan with acceptance. He feels amazing like this, and it hits that perfect spot in a whole new way.

My release builds and he tugs my hair, pulling my head back where he can lean down to kiss my neck. That's all I need to let it all escape. My pussy molds down around his dick and my release milks his all at the same time. We come together and it is the most beautiful moment, full of love.

"I want to worship your body every day, Maggie." Logan says as he rolls us over on our backs and pulls me into him.

I let my breathing catch up and I look at him, "Such a gentleman." I kiss him on the cheek and lean into him, resting on his chest. His arm drapes around me and I feel safe, secure, and warm.

I wonder if this is the kind of love my biological parents had.

We lay in the bed, silent for a moment, and then he looks down at me, "Have you talked to your parents?"

I shake my head and tears fill my eyes. I am unsure if I have finished processing everything. I still have love in my heart for them, but I am also hurt and disappointed that they have lied to me for so long. I always felt different growing up. Like something didn't fit. My whole personality was different from theirs. Maybe that's why I have always tried to win their approval in different ways. I even agreed to marry Stephen because I knew that is what they wanted for the family, and their image. I never loved him, though. Not really. It was all to please my parents.

Now that I know the truth, I feel robbed of the life I could have had and the people I could have loved. And I'm not so sure I can forgive someone so easily for taking that away from me.

Logan lifts my chin to his and kisses me softly. "I'll support whatever decision you make." He kisses my forehead.

"I think my dad sent me to you. My biological dad." I smile at him.

He smiles back, "Well, when we get there someday, I'll be sure to thank him."

Tears fill my eyes.

To be so devilish in bed, he is an angel to my heart.

24

I am standing at the kitchen sink looking out across my father's land *–my land*. Another week has passed, and I have talked to Logan a lot about my plans for all of it. I want us to build a house in the back pasture so I can sit on the back porch and watch the sunset over the pond. He loves the idea and we both hope it can be built soon, pending getting all of the breeding plans up and going. I am going into town today to see my grandparents and talk over some decisions Logan and I have made about the farm with Megan. I know she left it to us for now to take care of, but it wouldn't feel right keeping her out of the loop. This was her farm, first. Way before I ever came along. Even if we never found out we were cousins, she is still one of my best friends and I always want to keep her perspective on all the changes and plans, out of respect.

Logan has stayed with me in the farmhouse since they have been gone so much. It's just easier and honestly, we have had sex so much it's just nice to fall asleep in bed together. We even have our daily routine alongside each other every day; Breakfast, chores, showers, sex, dinner, sex, then sleep.

I think back to that scared girl who just up and left the life she knew with a broken heart and ended up in one of the best places she could dream of. How much life has changed, how much stronger I am now because of being here. I was broken, and this place – these people – mended me and added to much more than I could have ever imagined, when I arrived. Logan's statement to me still rings in my ears, *nothing's random.* How true that has been.

"Maggie." Logan runs into the house startling me. "We've got to go." He is out of breath like he ran the whole way from the barn.

I look confused and grab the papers off the table and Logan takes them out of my arms and throws them on the table, "You won't need those. Let's go." There is an uneasiness in his voice. He grabs my hand and pulls me out of the house and towards his truck. Nerves run over me.

"What's going on Logan?" I ask him, but he won't look at me.

We ride in silence, but I notice we are driving in the direction of the nursing home.

No. My heart starts to beat more rapidly in my chest in anticipation for the worst. Logan grips the steering wheel so tight; his knuckles are white.

***

Logan pulls in the front of the building, and we rush out of the truck. He grabs my hand and we both walk quickly to the front door. The receptionist I met a few weeks ago who hugged me gets up when she sees us and tears fill her eyes, "Maggie," she points to the door, "Don't worry about a name badge. Go." I smile at her, and fear fills my gut.

Logan holds my hand as we walk down the hall and as we get close to the front desk, I see the staff is wiping tears. Becky sees me first and she runs up to me, "Oh, Maggie." She hugs me, "Megan…" and I feel a hand on my back. It's Megan, and her eyes are puffy. She's been sobbing, and when she gets to me, her voice breaks.

"Collin and I didn't come visit this morning." She starts trying to hold back tears, "We met with their lawyer to make sure everything was secure for their estates, etc. I wanted to make sure you were still on everything, too." A single tear slides down her cheek and she looks down at our feet and then back up at me.

"Becky called me, and I called Logan to get you here as fast as possible, but they were gone before we even got here."

I search her fast realizing what she is saying, "No." my voice breaks and tears fall down my face.

Megan grabs my hand and leads me down the hall towards their room. She opens the door and I see Collin in a chair with his head down in his hands. Logan goes to him, and Collin stands when he sees us, throwing his arms around Logan.

The room is dimly lit, the tv is on low and their breakfast trays are untouched. I look over at the bed and my heart shatters into so many pieces. My grandparents are laying together in one bed, arms around each other and look so peaceful. They are holding hands and look like they are just sleeping. Margaret is still in her night gown and Jefferey is in pajama pants and a T-shirt. They both have smiles on their faces and if my mind is not playing tricks on me, it looks like they may have been in a deep conversation before they passed.

"Becky said they had laid down to take a nap." She wipes a tear and pulls me into her, wrapping her arm around my shoulder, "I knew they were slowly declining, but I didn't realize it was going to be this soon." I lay my head down on her shoulder and we both cry together for a while. Collin walks up beside Megan and wraps his arm around us.

"They have been through so much together." I start to say and wipe a tear as it falls, "From the military, losing their children, losing their grandchild, raising grandchildren, Jefferey getting sick-" I pause grasping the words I'm looking for, "then, they are reunited and get to leave this earth together, hand in hand. It's beautiful."

Logan comes up beside me and wraps his arm around me. I look up at him and see a tear fall down his face. "They took me in when I was at my lowest and had no one." He says in a low, sad tone.

We all stand there together, looking at the people who taught us so much about life. More than I am sure they realized.

A moment passes and Megan turns to me, "Oh," she says pulling a paper from her pocket, "Grandma must have been having a good day and knew this day was coming. She wrote us all notes. I found them in her Bible."

She hands me a piece of paper and I look at her, surprised.

Walking over to the chair Collin was sitting in, I sit down and open it. It's a handwritten note in pen.

My Magnolia,

My time on this earth is coming to an end. I can feel it in my soul. I'll be reunited with my children soon and how I cannot wait to see their faces and hug their necks. What I am going to miss is the time I could be spending with you. I don't have these good days often so while I'm in a state of mind to remember, I want to write this to you.

I always prayed for your return, and you would take over the farm like your father intended you to. Now I'm just sad to say I won't have an earthly seat to it. I'll be smiling from heaven.

You came into our life again as a girl just trying to get away from a bad situation and a life she didn't want for herself. A girl named Ivy. I knew from the moment I met you, there was something about you that drew me to you. You reminded me of, well, me. Your strength and the ability you had to dodge curve balls, even on the farm, and the help you gave us.

I know you must be having so many feelings. So many questions. And while I won't be here to answer them for you, I hope you read the books I've written to you over the years in full. There are so many life lessons in there and I hope they serve you well.

I know you must be so angry with your adoptive parents. I know because I would be angry, too. I wouldn't want to forgive them for taking time away from me. But honey, you don't forgive them for their sake, you forgive them for yours. You won't be able to truly move on with the life you want if you don't forgive those who wrong you along the way.

I love you, Maggie. I always have and I always will. You were the first to make me a grandmother and I will never forget the happiness you brought into our lives. You are the reason for our Magnolia Farm.

Please keep your cousins close. Let them teach you and help you. The only reason we never told them about you is because I didn't want them to experience the same heart break as we did. You are all my greatest joys in life other than my own children.

If you and Logan decide to make it official, make sure he continues to date you even when you're twenty years into marriage and have children running around. Always put each other first, communicate often and don't sweat even the smallest thing. This life is too short. Believe me. It comes and goes as fast as a blink. Enjoy every moment, even the bad.

And dodge those curve balls.

I love you more than you will ever know, Maggie.

Continue to go out and do big things.

And dodge those curve balls.

All my love,

Nana

I notice my chin is like a water fountain as the tears run down it, soaking my shirt and some of the paper I am reading. Logan is standing beside me for support, but he lets me have my moment.

Becky opens the door to their room and says, "Are y'all ready?" I stand up and Megan looks at me and I nod.

Megan takes my hand, and we walk out the door with Collin and Logan behind us as the funeral home staff goes into their room.

Becky hugs Megan and I, "Girls, if you ever need anything, please call me." She wipes a tear, and we thank her. She continues inside the room to help the funeral home staff. Megan and I walk towards the exit and to our trucks. Turning to her I smile, "Well, I know what we do now." And she cocks an eyebrow at me.

I grin, "We dodge this curve ball and continue the legacy."

We both wipe tears, and she smiles at me nodding her head agreeing.

Epilogue
A year later

I have officially changed all my legal papers back to Maggie Mapleson this past year and transferred Nana's Diner fully into mine and Megan's name. My cousin, and partner in crime.

"Maggie!" Logan calls from the front door. I look up at him.

"Want to go for a ride?" he asks me with a flirty smile.

I grin and get up from the table, pull my boots on at the front door and walk out on the porch with him. He knows my favorite thing to do, lately, is going on our evening rides.

Walking into the barn, Tiny's head sticks out, greeting me from his stall. I rub his nose, "Let's go for a ride, Bud." I grab his halter and tie it around him before opening his stall door.

Logan does the same with his mare and ties her beside Tiny while we saddle them up.

"Where to today?" I ask him, slinging my saddle on Tiny's back.

Logan's silent for a minute and clears his throat, "I was thinking the back pasture, near the pond."

I smile, thinking about the Magnolia Tree. I loved it before, but now knowing its purpose, it is now my favorite spot on the farm.

We mount our horses and walk off into the pasture that leads to the pond. Logan is quiet most of the ride.

Tiny prances a little as if something spooks him and his ears shoot forward, hearing something ahead of us.

Tiny trots up the hill and Logan follows behind. I'm concerned that a calf is out, or a coyote may be out here.

Coming over the top of the hill I see Megan's truck parked at the Magnolia Tree and I get excited. "Are we going swimming?" I ask Logan with a grin, and he just grins back at me.

I break Tiny into a lope and head towards the pond. The wind blowing through my hair is the best feeling with Tiny moving steadily under me. The green grass blows all around me but the pond water is as still as it can be when I get up to it. The Magnolia Tree leaves move just a little as the slight breeze blows.

Megan and Collin smile at me as I dismount Tiny and let him eat the grass by the dock as I hug them. They hug me back and Logan comes riding up behind us. He dismounts his mare and lets her graze beside Tiny.

"You guys ready to go swimming?" I ask, looking at them.

They both look at each other confused and then back at Logan.

He lets out a cough and grabs my hand. I look at him confused, and he leads me away from Megan and Collin, towards the edge of the dock.

That's when I notice it. There are flags placed out in the middle of the land towards the back side of the pond where I plan to build someday. My eyes widen and look at him but my voice hitches.

"Magnolia Rose Mapleson," Logan says as he gets down on one knee. "A while back, I told you nothing is random, and you didn't believe me at first. But you see, I believed it the moment my eyes met yours at Hilltop." We both grin at the memory.

He rubs his thumb over my hand and looks back up at me, "I'm not going to say I'm going to make all your dreams come true because, let's face it, you are hard-headed enough to not want help." I laugh at the truth in that statement. "But I do want to be the one beside you when all your dreams come true." He pulls out a box from his back pocket. "Will you marry me?"

I gasp and tears fill my eyes. "Y-yes!" I squeal and he picks me up, spinning me around. I hear Collin "hoot hooting" in the background and Megan is jumping up and down. Logan puts the ring on my finger and they both run down to the dock and meet us. Collin picks me up and spins me around in a hug! "I never dreamed the girl who was so rude to me at the restaurant that day would be my neighbor…and cousin." He laughs at the last part and Megan comes over and hugs me.

"Oh," Logan says as Megan and I pull out of our hug and he takes my hand, "Welcome home, Maggie." He kisses my forehead. "We break ground next week." Tears fill my eyes, and I couldn't be happier.

On this farm, with my family.

Epilogue
Five years later

I bend down, patting Tiny on the neck. He still makes every pasture check with me. Reba, Izzy and George take every step as well. I sit on top of our mountain and look around and down at our kingdom below. It is cooler outside this time of the year as fall is in the air. The trees are turning beautiful shades of orange, yellow and red. It's honestly my favorite time of the year.

The wind blows just enough that mine and Tiny's hair floats in it, effortlessly. Mine and Logan's home is perfect. A beautiful, white farmhouse, just like we both love, in the perfect spot. I have pictured that house in that exact location since the first time I visited the pond.

We still swim in the pond often, and Collin stays in the main farmhouse.

Megan was so happy with the way her favorite colt, Crackerjack, was doing that she decided to geld him and enter the rodeo circuit to get back into barrel racing and roping. She is not at home as much and that is a bummer, but we talk often on the phone. She sends me videos of her runs every chance she gets. When we break our colts, she will train them on certain events and sell them while she is on the road.

Logan and I continued with the plans we agreed on for the breeding program, and it has been a grand success. So successful that Rylee's ranch has reached out a time or two to do business with us.

I took my Nana's advice and decided to forgive Rylee for the way she treated me that day in her barn. We work with them closely now and have been successful getting our bloodlines out into the world.

I also forgave my parents. I did not want to at first, but after reading Nana's words the day they passed, I knew she was right. No matter how much I did not want to admit it- I am seeing more of her traits in me as the days pass.

I do not see my parents often, but they did show up for our wedding. We had it on the farm, of course, a year after Logan proposed. I wanted it to be on the pond under the Magnolia Tree. Four red Cardinals stayed for the whole ceremony and then flew away as Logan and I exited on horseback. Some may believe otherwise, but I would like to think they were my parents and grandparents, present for my big day.

My father walked me down the aisle and it was a bittersweet moment as he gave me away to Logan. He is the man of my dreams. This man still gives me butterflies at how he loves and appreciates me both physically and mentally. I think I finally have the love my biological parents and grandparents talked about.

I hear hoof beats coming up the hill and see Logan as his mare tops it. He is the most handsome man I have ever laid eyes on and sometimes, I have to pinch myself to remember that he is mine. He is wearing his cap backwards and a sleeveless t-shirt with his dirty jeans.

"Hey my girl." He says as he rides up beside Tiny and I, kissing me on the cheek.

I am a basket of emotions as I look over the mountains below us. I do not look at him. Instead, I take deep breaths to calm my nerves.

"Maggie?" he searches me, "Is everything okay?" he asks, looking nervous.

I smile and turn to him reaching into my pocket and pulling out a pregnancy test. He sees it and his eyes widen, "Maggie?!" He searches my eyes and tears fill his.

"We can't dodge this curve ball." I laugh and he pulls me into him, kissing me fiercely.

Acknowledgement

To my husband, for believing in me. You watched me for years not believing in myself but yet you never waved in your support. Thank you for reading countless chapters for me when I needed fresh eyes and sacrificing many nights in the bed alone while I stayed up all night writing. If anyone understands my obsession with falling in love with fictional people and places, its you. I love you.

To my mother, for the sacrifices you have made throughout my entire life. Until Deddy came along, it was just you and me. Though I didn't know it as a child, I know now the sacrifices you made for me. Thank you. I will always cherish the late-night laughs and the "Jess we got to stop talking so I can go to sleep" giggles.

To Deddy, for being the dad you didn't have to be. I don't know where my mom and I would be if you and my siblings never came into our life. Thank you for always treating me as more than just your stepdaughter. You are and will forever be my Deddy.

To my sister-in-law and brother-in-law for being amazing models for book content. You guys seriously don't know how much you mean to us. Our village is priceless and we are so grateful for it.

To my nieces, when your older, I hope you read this and understand the importance in the meaning behind this book. I hope you dodge all the curve balls thrown at you and I hope you never let a man make you forget your worth.

To my ARC and Beta readers, thank you for taking time out of your busy lives to read my story and give me a chance. I cherish our friendship more than you know and I cannot wait for all the future books you will have the first opportunity to read for me. This book would not have been possible without you.

To my editor, Stevi, thank you for correcting the southerner out of my words. You are more than my editor; you are my friend and I think the world of you. Knowing you for as long as I have, I never would have dreamed we would be doing this together someday. Thank you for supporting me. Love you bunches!

To baby Jessie, you and I have been through a lot together. A lot of tears and a lot of unknowns. We always knew there was not anything wrong with us. We just have a big imagination and heart to fit. We always knew we were bigger than our circumstances and dodged each curve ball, no matter the punch it had, and kept going. I will forever be thankful for your hard head, stubbornness, and personality. It may have kept our circle small but in the end, it has been a saving grace. Hang on sister, this ride is only the beginning.

About The Author

Jessica is closer to this book than you realize. She grew up riding horses and barrel racing. She and her sister shared a barn full of horses together in their small town. Many weekends were full of a loaded down horse trailer and a truck full of friends.

Her grandparents house had a big Magnolia Tree she grew up climbing with her cousins in their yard.

Now days her and her husband love spending time on the lake, tending to their animals, and gardening.

Read more about Jessica: www.authorjdwhaley.com

Instagram: https://www.instagram.com/jessicawhaleybooks/
Facebook: Jessica Whaley – Author

Did you love Maggie's story?

 Please leave a review on Amazon and Goodreads!

Coming Soon!

Megan's story will pick up where Maggie's ends! Releasing soon in 2024!

Subscribe to Jessica's newsletter HERE to be the first to know when it will release! Also located on her website!